Their Silver Wedding Journey

Volume 3

William Dean Howells

Alpha Editions

This edition published in 2023

ISBN : 9789357941044

Design and Setting By
Alpha Editions
www.alphaedis.com
Email - info@alphaedis.com

VOLUME 3

PART III.

XLVIII.

At the first station where the train stopped, a young German bowed himself into the compartment with the Marches, and so visibly resisted an impulse to smoke that March begged him to light his cigarette. In the talk which this friendly overture led to between them he explained that he was a railway architect, employed by the government on that line of road, and was travelling officially. March spoke of Nuremberg; he owned the sort of surfeit he had suffered from its excessive mediaevalism, and the young man said it was part of the new imperial patriotism to cherish the Gothic throughout Germany; no other sort of architecture was permitted in Nuremberg. But they would find enough classicism at Ansbach, he promised them, and he entered with sympathetic intelligence into their wish to see this former capital when March told him they were going to stop there, in hopes of something typical of the old disjointed Germany of the petty principalities, the little paternal despotisms now extinct.

As they talked on, partly in German and partly in English, their purpose in visiting Ansbach appeared to the Marches more meditated than it was. In fact it was somewhat accidental; Ansbach was near Nuremberg; it was not much out of the way to Holland. They took more and more credit to themselves for a reasoned and definite motive, in the light of their companion's enthusiasm for the place, and its charm began for them with the drive from the station through streets whose sentiment was both Italian and French, and where there was a yellowish cast in the gray of the architecture which was almost Mantuan. They rested their sensibilities, so bruised and fretted by Gothic angles and points, against the smooth surfaces of the prevailing classicistic facades of the houses as they passed, and when they arrived at their hotel, an old mansion of Versailles type, fronting on a long irregular square planted with pollard sycamores, they said that it might as well have been Lucca.

The archway and stairway of the hotel were draped with the Bavarian colors, and they were obscurely flattered to learn that Prince Leopold, the brother of the Prince-Regent of the kingdom, had taken rooms there, on his way to the manoeuvres at Nuremberg, and was momently expected with his suite. They realized that they were not of the princely party, however, when they were told that he had sole possession of the dining-room, and they went out to another hotel, and had their supper in keeping delightfully native. People seemed to come there to write their letters and make up their accounts, as well as to eat their suppers; they called for stationery like characters in old comedy, and the clatter of crockery and the scratching of pens went on together; and fortune offered the Marches a delicate reparation for their exclusion from their own hotel in the cold popular reception of the prince which they got back just in time to witness. A very small group of people, mostly women and boys, had gathered to see him arrive, but there was no cheering or any sign of public interest. Perhaps he personally merited none; he looked a dull, sad man, with his plain, stubbed features; and after he had mounted to his apartment, the officers of his staff stood quite across the landing, and barred the passage of the Americans, ignoring even Mrs. March's presence, as they talked together.

"Well, my dear," said her husband, "here you have it at last. This is what you've been living for, ever since we came to Germany. It's a great moment."

"Yes. What are you going to do?"

"Who? I? Oh, nothing! This is your affair; it's for you to act."

If she had been young, she might have withered them with a glance; she doubted now if her dim eyes would have any such power; but she advanced steadily upon them, and then the officers seemed aware of her, and stood aside.

March always insisted that they stood aside apologetically, but she held as firmly that they stood aside impertinently, or at least indifferently, and that the insult to her American womanhood was perfectly ideal. It is true that nothing of the kind happened again during their stay at the hotel; the prince's officers were afterwards about in the corridors and on the stairs, but they offered no shadow of obstruction to her going and coming, and the landlord himself was not so preoccupied with his highhotes but he had time to express his grief that she had been obliged to go out for supper.

They satisfied the passion for the little obsolete capital which had been growing upon them by strolling past the old Resident at an hour so favorable for a first impression. It loomed in the gathering dusk even vaster than it was, and it was really vast enough for the pride of a King of France, much more a Margrave of Ansbach. Time had blackened and blotched its coarse limestone walls to one complexion with the statues swelling and strutting in the figure of Roman legionaries before it, and standing out against the evening sky along its balustraded roof, and had softened to the right tint the stretch of half a dozen houses with mansard roofs and renaissance facades obsequiously in keeping with the Versailles ideal of a Resident. In the rear, and elsewhere at fit distance from its courts, a native architecture prevailed; and at no great remove the Marches found themselves in a simple German town again. There they stumbled upon a little bookseller's shop blinking in a quiet corner, and bought three or four guides and small histories of Ansbach, which they carried home, and studied between drowsing and waking. The wonderful German syntax seems at its most enigmatical in this sort of literature, and sometimes they lost themselves in its labyrinths completely, and only made their way perilously out with the help of cumulative declensions, past articles and adjectives blindly seeking their nouns, to long-procrastinated verbs dancing like swamp-fires in the distance. They emerged a little less ignorant than they went in, and better qualified than they would otherwise have been for their second visit to the Schloss, which they paid early the next morning.

They were so early, indeed, that when they mounted from the great inner court, much too big for Ansbach, if not for the building, and rung the custodian's bell, a smiling maid who let them into an ante-room, where she kept on picking over vegetables for her dinner, said the custodian was busy, and could not be seen till ten o'clock. She seemed, in her nook of the pretentious pile, as innocently unconscious of its history as any hen-sparrow who had built her nest in some coign of its architecture; and her friendly, peaceful domesticity remained a wholesome human background to the tragedies and comedies of the past, and held them in a picturesque relief in which they were alike tolerable and even charming.

The history of Ansbach strikes its roots in the soil of fable, and above ground is a gnarled and twisted growth of good and bad from the time of the Great Charles to the time of the Great Frederick. Between these times she had her various rulers, ecclesiastical and secular, in various forms of vassalage to the empire; but for nearly four centuries her sovereignty was in the hands of the margraves, who reigned in a constantly increasing splendor till the last sold her outright to the King of Prussia in 1791, and went to live in England on the proceeds. She had taken her part in the miseries and glories of the wars that desolated Germany, but after the Reformation, when she turned from the ancient faith to which she owed her cloistered origin under St. Gumpertus, her people had peace except when their last prince sold them to fight the battles of others. It is in this last transaction that her history, almost in the moment when she ceased to have a history of her own, links to that of the modern world, and that it came home to the Marches in their national character; for two thousand of those poor Ansbach mercenaries were bought up by England and sent to put down a rebellion in her American colonies.

Humanly, they were more concerned for the Last Margrave, because of certain qualities which made him the Best Margrave, in spite of the defects of his qualities. He was the son of the Wild Margrave, equally known in the Ansbach annals, who may not have been the Worst Margrave, but who had certainly a bad trick of putting his subjects to death without trial, and in cases where there was special haste, with his own hand. He sent his son to the university at Utrecht because he believed that the republican influences in Holland would be wholesome for him, and then he sent him to travel in Italy; but when the boy came home looking frail and sick, the Wild Margrave charged his official travelling companion with neglect, and had the unhappy

Hofrath Meyer hanged without process for this crime. One of the gentlemen of his realm, for a pasquinade on the Margrave, was brought to the scaffold; he had, at various times, twenty-two of his soldiers shot with arrows and bullets or hanged for desertion, besides many whose penalties his clemency commuted to the loss of an ear or a nose; a Hungarian who killed his hunting-dog, he had broken alive on the wheel. A soldier's wife was hanged for complicity in a case of desertion; a young soldier who eloped with the girl he loved was brought to Ansbach from a neighboring town, and hanged with her on the same gallows. A sentry at the door of one of the Margrave's castles amiably complied with the Margrave's request to let him take his gun for a moment, on the pretence of wishing to look at it. For this breach of discipline the prince covered him with abuse and gave him over to his hussars, who bound him to a horse's tail and dragged him through the streets; he died of his injuries. The kennel-master who had charge of the Margrave's dogs was accused of neglecting them: without further inquiry the Margrave rode to the man's house and shot him down on his own threshold. A shepherd who met the Margrave on a shying horse did not get his flock out of the way quickly enough; the Margrave demanded the pistols of a gentleman in his company, but he answered that they were not loaded, and the shepherd's life was saved. As they returned home the gentleman fired them off. "What does that mean?" cried the Margrave, furiously. "It means, gracious lord, that you will sleep sweeter tonight, for not having heard my pistols an hour sooner."

From this it appears that the gracious lord had his moments of regret; but perhaps it is not altogether strange that when he died, the whole population "stormed through the streets to meet his funeral train, not in awe-stricken silence to meditate on the fall of human grandeur, but to unite in an eager tumult of rejoicing, as if some cruel brigand who had long held the city in terror were delivered over to them bound and in chains." For nearly thirty years this blood-stained miscreant had reigned over his hapless people in a sovereign plenitude of power, which by the theory of German imperialism in our day is still a divine right.

They called him the Wild Margrave, in their instinctive revolt from the belief that any man not untamably savage could be guilty of his atrocities; and they called his son the Last Margrave, with a touch of the poetry which perhaps records a regret for their extinction as a state. He did not harry them as his father had done; his mild rule was the effect partly of the indifference and distaste for his country bred, by his long sojourns abroad; but doubtless also it was the effect of a kindly nature. Even in the matter of selling a few thousands of them to fight the battles of a bad cause on the other side of the world, he had the best of motives, and faithfully applied the proceeds to the payment of the state debt and the embellishment of the capital.

His mother was a younger sister of Frederick the Great, and was so constantly at war with her husband that probably she had nothing to do with the marriage which the Wild Margrave forced upon their son. Love certainly had nothing to do with it, and the Last Margrave early escaped from it to the society of Mlle. Clairon, the great French tragedienne, whom he met in Paris, and whom he persuaded to come and make her home with him in Ansbach. She lived there seventeen years, and though always an alien, she bore herself with kindness to all classes, and is still remembered there by the roll of butter which calls itself a Klarungswecke in its imperfect French.

No roll of butter records in faltering accents the name of the brilliant and disdainful English lady who replaced this poor tragic muse in the Margrave's heart, though the lady herself lived to be the last Margravine of Ansbach, where everybody seems to have hated her with a passion which she doubtless knew how to return. She was the daughter of the Earl of Berkeley, and the wife of Lord Craven, a sufficiently unfaithful and unworthy nobleman by her account, from whom she was living apart when the Margrave asked her to his capital. There she set herself to oust Mlle. Clairon with sneers and jests for the theatrical style which the actress could not outlive. Lady Craven said she was sure Clairon's nightcap must be a crown of gilt paper; and when Clairon threatened to kill herself, and the Margrave was alarmed, "You forget," said Lady Craven, "that actresses only stab themselves under their sleeves."

She drove Clairon from Ansbach, and the great tragedienne returned to Paris, where she remained true to her false friend, and from time to time wrote him letters full of magnanimous counsel and generous tenderness. But she could not have been so good company as Lady Craven, who was a very gifted person, and knew how to compose songs and sing them, and write comedies and play them, and who could keep the Margrave amused in many ways. When his loveless and childless wife died he married the English woman, but he grew more and more weary of his dull little court and his dull little country, and after a while, considering the uncertain tenure sovereigns had of their heads since the French King had lost his, and the fact that he had no heirs to follow him in his principality, he resolved to cede it for a certain sum to Prussia. To this end his new wife's urgence was perhaps not wanting. They went to England, where she outlived him ten years, and wrote her memoirs.

The custodian of the Schloss came at last, and the Marches saw instantly that he was worth waiting for. He was as vainglorious of the palace as any grand-monarching margrave of them all. He could not have been more personally superb in showing their different effigies if they had been his own family portraits, and he would not spare the strangers a single splendor of the twenty vast, handsome, tiresome, Versailles-like rooms he led them through. The rooms were fatiguing physically, but so poignantly interesting that Mrs.

March would not have missed, though she perished of her pleasure, one of the things she saw. She had for once a surfeit of highhoting in the pictures, the porcelains, the thrones and canopies, the tapestries, the historical associations with the margraves and their marriages, with the Great Frederick and the Great Napoleon. The Great Napoleon's man Bernadotte made the Schloss his headquarters when he occupied Ansbach after Austerlitz, and here he completed his arrangements for taking her bargain from Prussia and handing it over to Bavaria, with whom it still remains. Twice the Great Frederick had sojourned in the palace; visiting his sister Louise, the wife of the Wild Margrave, and more than once it had welcomed her next neighbor and sister Wilhelmina, the Margravine of Baireuth, whose autobiographic voice, piercingly plaintive and reproachful, seemed to quiver in the air. Here, oddly enough, the spell of the Wild Margrave weakened in the presence of his portrait, which signally failed to justify his fame of furious tyrant. That seems, indeed, to have been rather the popular and historical conception of him than the impression he made upon his exalted contemporaries. The Margravine of Baireuth at any rate could so far excuse her poor blood-stained brother-in-law as to say: "The Margrave of Ansbach . . . was a young prince who had been very badly educated. He continually ill-treated my sister; they led the life of cat and dog. My sister, it is true, was sometimes in fault . . . . Her education had been very bad. . . She was married at fourteen."

At parting, the custodian told the Marches that he would easily have known them for Americans by the handsome fee they gave him; they came away flown with his praise; and their national vanity was again flattered when they got out into the principal square of Ansbach. There, in a bookseller's window, they found among the pamphlets teaching different languages without a master, one devoted to the Amerikanische Sprache as distinguished from the Englische Sprache. That there could be no mistake, the cover was printed with colors in a German ideal of the star-spangled banner; and March said he always knew that we had a language of our own, and that now he was going in to buy that pamphlet and find out what it was like. He asked the young shop-woman how it differed from English, which she spoke fairly well from having lived eight years in Chicago. She said that it differed from the English mainly in emphasis and pronunciation. "For instance, the English say 'HALF past', and the Americans 'Half PAST'; the English say 'laht' and the Americans say 'late'."

The weather had now been clear quite long enough, and it was raining again, a fine, bitter, piercing drizzle. They asked the girl if it always rained in Ansbach; and she owned that it nearly always did. She said that sometimes she longed for a little American summer; that it was never quite warm in Ansbach; and when they had got out into the rain, March said: "It was very nice to stumble on Chicago in an Ansbach book-store. You ought to have told her you had a married daughter in Chicago. Don't miss another such chance."

"We shall need another bag if we keep on buying books at this rate," said his wife with tranquil irrelevance; and not to give him time for protest; she pushed him into a shop where the valises in the window perhaps suggested her thought. March made haste to forestall her there by saying they were Americans, but the mistress of the shop seemed to have her misgivings, and "Born Americans, perhaps?" she ventured. She had probably never met any but the naturalized sort, and supposed these were the only sort. March reassured her, and then she said she had a son living in Jersey City, and she made March take his address that he might tell him he had seen his mother; she had apparently no conception what a great way Jersey City is from New York.

Mrs. March would not take his arm when they came out. "Now, that is what I never can get used to in you, Basil, and I've tried to palliate it for twenty-seven years. You know you won't look up that poor woman's son! Why did you let her think you would?"

"How could I tell her I wouldn't? Perhaps I shall."

"No, no! You never will. I know you're good and kind, and that's why I can't understand your being so cruel. When we get back, how will you ever find time to go over to Jersey City?"

He could not tell, but at last he said: "I'll tell you what! You must keep me up to it. You know how much you enjoy making me do my duty, and this will be such a pleasure!"

She laughed forlornly, but after a moment she took his arm; and he began, from the example of this good mother, to philosophize the continuous simplicity and sanity of the people of Ansbach under all their civic changes. Saints and soldiers, knights and barons, margraves, princes, kings, emperors, had come and gone, and left their single-hearted, friendly subjectfolk pretty much what they found them. The people had suffered and survived through a thousand wars, and apparently prospered on under all governments and misgovernments. When the court was most French, most artificial, most vicious, the citizen life must have remained immutably German, dull, and kind. After all, he said, humanity seemed everywhere to be pretty safe, and pretty much the same.

"Yes, that is all very well," she returned, "and you can theorize interestingly enough; but I'm afraid that poor mother, there, had no more reality for you than those people in the past. You appreciate her as a type, and you don't care for her as a human being. You're nothing but a dreamer, after all. I don't blame you," she went on. "It's your temperament, and you can't change, now."

"I may change for the worse," he threatened. "I think I have, already. I don't believe I could stand up to Dryfoos, now, as I did for poor old Lindau, when I risked your bread and butter for his. I look back in wonder and admiration at myself. I've steadily lost touch with life since then. I'm a trifler, a dilettante, and an amateur of the right and the good as I used to be when I was young. Oh, I have the grace to be troubled at times, now, and once I never was. It never occurred to me then that the world wasn't made to interest me, or at the best to instruct me, but it does, now, at times."

She always came to his defence when he accused himself; it was the best ground he could take with her. "I think you behaved very well with Burnamy. You did your duty then."

"Did I? I'm not so sure. At any rate, it's the last time I shall do it. I've served my term. I think I should tell him that he was all right in that business with Stoller, if I were to meet him, now."

"Isn't it strange," she said, provisionally, "that we don't come upon a trace of him anywhere in Ansbach?"

"Ah, you've been hoping he would turn up!"

"Yes. I don't deny it. I feel very unhappy about him."

"I don't. He's too much like me. He would have been quite capable of promising that poor woman to look up her son in Jersey City. When I think of that, I have no patience with Burnamy."

"I am going to ask the landlord about him, now he's got rid of his highhotes," said Mrs. March.

XLIX.

They went home to their hotel for their midday dinner, and to the comfort of having it nearly all to themselves. Prince Leopold had risen early, like all the hard-working potentates of the continent, and got away to the manoeuvres somewhere at six o'clock; the decorations had been removed, and the court-yard where the hired coach and pair of the prince had rolled in the evening before had only a few majestic ducks waddling about in it and quacking together, indifferent to the presence of a yellow mail-wagon, on which the driver had been apparently dozing till the hour of noon should sound. He sat there immovable, but at the last stroke of the clock he woke up and drove vigorously away to the station.

The dining-room which they had been kept out of by the prince the night before was not such as to embitter the sense of their wrong by its splendor. After all, the tastes of royalty must be simple, if the prince might have gone to the Schloss and had chosen rather to stay at this modest hotel; but perhaps the Schloss was reserved for more immediate royalty than the brothers of prince-regents; and in that case he could not have done better than dine at the Golden Star. If he paid no more than two marks, he dined as cheaply as a prince could wish, and as abundantly. The wine at Ansbach was rather thin and sour, but the bread, March declared, was the best bread in the whole world, not excepting the bread of Carlsbad.

After dinner the Marches had some of the local pastry, not so incomparable as the bread, with their coffee, which they had served them in a pavilion of the beautiful garden remaining to the hotel from the time when it was a patrician mansion. The garden had roses in it and several sorts of late summer flowers, as well as ripe cherries, currants, grapes, and a Virginia-creeper red with autumn, all harmoniously contemporaneous, as they might easily be in a climate where no one of the seasons can very well know itself from the others. It had not been raining for half an hour, and the sun was scalding hot, so that the shelter of their roof was very grateful, and the puddles of the paths were drying up with the haste which puddles have to make in Germany, between rains, if they are ever going to dry up at all.

The landlord came out to see if they were well served, and he was sincerely obliging in the English he had learned as a waiter in London. Mrs. March made haste to ask him if a young American of the name of Burnamy had been staying with him a few weeks before; and she described Burnamy's beauty and amiability so vividly that the landlord, if he had been a woman, could not have failed to remember him. But he failed, with a real grief, apparently, and certainly a real politeness, to recall either his name or his person. The landlord was an intelligent, good-looking young fellow; he told them that he was lately married, and they liked him so much that they were sorry to see him afterwards privately boxing the ears of the piccolo, the waiter's little understudy. Perhaps the piccolo deserved it, but they would rather not have witnessed his punishment; his being in a dress-coat seemed to make it also an indignity.

In the late afternoon they went to the cafe in the old Orangery of the Schloss for a cup of tea, and found themselves in the company of several Ansbach ladies who had brought their work, in the evident habit of coming there every afternoon for their coffee and for a dish of gossip. They were kind, uncomely, motherly-looking bodies; one of them combed her hair at the table; and they all sat outside of the cafe with their feet on the borders of the puddles which had not dried up there in the shade of the building.

A deep lawn, darkened at its farther edge by the long shadows of trees, stretched before them with the sunset light on it, and it was all very quiet and friendly. The tea brought to the Marches was brewed from some herb apparently of native growth, with bits of what looked like willow leaves in it, but it was flavored with a clove in each cup, and they sat contentedly over it and tried to make out what the Ansbach ladies were, talking about. These had recognized the strangers for Americans, and one of them explained that Americans spoke the same language as the English and yet were not quite the same people.

"She differs from the girl in the book-store," said March, translating to his wife. "Let us get away before she says that we are not so nice as the English," and they made off toward the avenue of trees beyond the lawn.

There were a few people walking up and down in the alley, making the most of the moment of dry weather. They saluted one another like acquaintances, and three clean-shaven, walnut-faced old peasants bowed in response to March's stare, with a self-respectful civility. They were yeomen of the region of Ansbach, where the country round about is dotted with their cottages, and not held in vast homeless tracts by the nobles as in North Germany.

The Bavarian who had imparted this fact to March at breakfast, not without a certain tacit pride in it to the disadvantage of the Prussians, was at the supper table, and was disposed to more talk, which he managed in a stout, slow English of his own. He said he had never really spoken English with an English-speaking person before, or at all since he studied it in school at Munich.

"I should be afraid to put my school-boy German against your English," March said, and, when he had understood, the other laughed for pleasure, and reported the compliment to his wife in their own parlance. "You Germans certainly beat us in languages."

"Oh, well," he retaliated, "the Americans beat us in some other things," and Mrs. March felt that this was but just; she would have liked to mention a few, but not ungraciously; she and the German lady kept smiling across the table, and trying detached vocables of their respective tongues upon each other.

The Bavarian said he lived in Munich still, but was in Ansbach on an affair of business; he asked March if he were not going to see the manoeuvres somewhere. Till now the manoeuvres had merely been the interesting background of their travel; but now, hearing that the Emperor of Germany, the King of Saxony, the Regent of Bavaria, and the King of Wurtemberg, the Grand-Dukes of Weimar and Baden, with visiting potentates of all sorts, and innumerable lesser highhotes, foreign and domestic, were to be present, Mrs. March resolved that they must go to at least one of the reviews.

"If you go to Frankfort, you can see the King of Italy too," said the Bavarian, but he owned that they probably could not get into a hotel there, and he asked why they should not go to Wurzburg, where they could see all the sovereigns except the King of Italy.

"Wurzburg? Wurzburg?" March queried of his wife. "Where did we hear of that place?"

"Isn't it where Burnamy said Mr. Stoller had left his daughters at school?"

"So it is! And is that on the way to the Rhine?" he asked the Bavarian.

"No, no! Wurzburg is on the Main, about five hours from Ansbach. And it is a very interesting place. It is where the good wine comes from."

"Oh, yes," said March, and in their rooms his wife got out all their guides and maps and began to inform herself and to inform him about Wurzburg. But first she said it was very cold and he must order some fire made in the tall German stove in their parlor. The maid who came said "Gleich," but she did not come back, and about the time they were getting furious at her neglect, they began getting warm. He put his hand on the stove and found it hot; then he looked down for a door in the stove where he might shut a damper; there was no door.

"Good heavens!" he shouted. "It's like something in a dream," and he ran to pull the bell for help.

"No, no! Don't ring! It will make us ridiculous. They'll think Americans don't know anything. There must be some way of dampening the stove; and if there isn't, I'd rather suffocate than give myself away." Mrs. March ran and opened the window, while her husband carefully examined the stove at every point, and explored the pipe for the damper in vain. "Can't you find it?" The night wind came in raw and damp, and threatened to blow their lamp out, and she was obliged to shut the window.

"Not a sign of it. I will go down and ask the landlord in strict confidence how they dampen their stoves in Ansbach."

"Well, if you must. It's getting hotter every moment." She followed him timorously into the corridor, lit by a hanging lamp, turned low for the night.

He looked at his watch; it was eleven o'clock. "I'm afraid they're all in bed."

"Yes; you mustn't go! We must try to find out for ourselves. What can that door be for?"

It was a low iron door, half the height of a man, in the wall near their room, and it yielded to his pull. "Get a candle," he whispered, and when she brought it, he stooped to enter the doorway.

"Oh, do you think you'd better?" she hesitated.

"You can come, too, if you're afraid. You've always said you wanted to die with me."

"Well. But you go first."

He disappeared within, and then came back to the doorway. "Just come in here, a moment." She found herself in a sort of antechamber, half the height of her own room, and following his gesture she looked down where in one corner some crouching monster seemed showing its fiery teeth in a grin of derision. This grin was the damper of their stove, and this was where the maid had kindled the fire which had been roasting them alive, and was still joyously chuckling to itself. "I think that Munich man was wrong. I don't believe we beat the Germans in anything. There isn't a hotel in the United States where the stoves have no front doors, and every one of them has the space of a good-sized flat given up to the convenience of kindling a fire in it."

L.

After a red sunset of shameless duplicity March was awakened to a rainy morning by the clinking of cavalry hoofs on the pavement of the long-irregular square before the hotel, and he hurried out to see the passing of the soldiers on their way to the manoeuvres. They were troops of all arms, but mainly infantry, and as they stumped heavily through the groups of apathetic citizens in their mud-splashed boots, they took the steady downpour on their dripping helmets. Some of them were smoking, but none smiling, except one gay fellow who made a joke to a serving-maid on the sidewalk. An old officer halted his staff to scold a citizen who had given him a mistaken direction. The shame of the erring man was great, and the pride of a fellow-citizen who corrected him was not less, though the arrogant brute before whom they both cringed used them with equal scorn; the younger officers listened indifferently round on horseback behind the glitter of their eyeglasses, and one of them amused himself by turning the silver bangles on his wrist.

Then the files of soldier slaves passed on, and March crossed the bridge spanning the gardens in what had been the city moat, and found his way to the market-place, under the walls of the old Gothic church of St. Gumpertus. The market, which spread pretty well over the square, seemed to be also a fair, with peasants' clothes and local pottery for sale, as well as fruits and vegetables, and large baskets of flowers, with old women squatting before them. It was all as picturesque as the markets used to be in Montreal and Quebec, and in a cloudy memory of his wedding journey long before, he bought so lavishly of the flowers to carry back to his wife that a little girl, who saw his arm-load from her window as he returned, laughed at him, and then drew shyly back. Her laugh reminded him how many happy children he had seen in Germany, and how freely they seemed to play everywhere, with no one to make them afraid. When they grow up the women laugh as little as the men, whose rude toil the soldiering leaves them to.

He got home with his flowers, and his wife took them absently, and made him join her in watching the sight which had fascinated her in the street under their windows. A slender girl, with a waist as slim as a corseted officer's, from time to time came out of the house across the way to the firewood which had been thrown from a wagon upon the sidewalk there. Each time she embraced several of the heavy four-foot logs and disappeared with them in-doors. Once she paused from her work to joke with a well-dressed man who came by; and seemed to find nothing odd in her work; some gentlemen lounging at the window over head watched her with no apparent sense of anomaly.

"What do you think of that?" asked Mrs. March. "I think it's good exercise for the girl, and I should like to recommend it to those fat fellows at the window. I suppose she'll saw the wood in the cellar, and then lug it up stairs, and pile it up in the stoves' dressing-rooms."

"Don't laugh! It's too disgraceful."

"Well, I don't know! If you like, I'll offer these gentlemen across the way your opinion of it in the language of Goethe and Schiller."

"I wish you'd offer my opinion of them. They've been staring in here with an opera-glass."

"Ah, that's a different affair. There isn't much going on in Ansbach, and they have to make the most of it."

The lower casements of the houses were furnished with mirrors set at right angles with them, and nothing which went on in the streets was lost. Some of the streets were long and straight, and at rare moments they lay full of sun. At such times the Marches were puzzled by the sight of citizens carrying open umbrellas, and they wondered if they had forgotten to put them down, or thought it not worth while in the brief respites from the rain, or were profiting by such rare occasions to dry them; and some other sights remained baffling to the last. Once a man with his hands pinioned before him, and a gendarme marching stolidly after him with his musket on his shoulder, passed under their windows; but who he was, or what he, had done, or was to suffer, they never knew. Another time a pair went by on the way to the railway station: a young man carrying an umbrella under his arm, and a very decent-looking old woman lugging a heavy carpet bag, who left them to the lasting question whether she was the young man's servant in her best clothes, or merely his mother.

Women do not do everything in Ansbach, however, the sacristans being men, as the Marches found when they went to complete their impression of the courtly past of the city by visiting the funeral chapel of the margraves in the crypt of St. Johannis Church. In the little ex-margravely capital there was something of the neighborly interest in the curiosity of strangers which endears Italian witness. The white-haired street-sweeper of Ansbach, who willingly left his broom to guide them to the house of the sacristan, might have been a street-sweeper in Vicenza; and the old sacristan, when he put his velvet skull-cap out of an upper window and professed his willingness to show them the chapel, disappointed them by saying "Gleich!" instead of "Subito!" The architecture of the houses was a party to the illusion. St. Johannis, like the older church of St. Gumpertus, is Gothic, with the two unequal towers which seem distinctive of Ansbach; at the St. Gumpertus end of the place where they both stand the dwellings are Gothic too, and might be in Hamburg; but at the St. Johannis end they seem to have felt the exotic spirit of the court, and are of a sort of Teutonized renaissance.

The rococo margraves and margravines used of course to worship in St. Johannis Church. Now they all, such as did not marry abroad, lie in the crypt of the church, in caskets of bronze and copper and marble, with draperies of black samite, more and more funereally vainglorious to the last. Their courtly coffins are ranged in a kind of hemicycle, with the little coffins of the children that died before they came to the knowledge of their greatness. On one of these a kneeling figurine in bronze holds up the effigy of the child within; on another the epitaph plays tenderly with the fate of a little princess, who died in her first year.

In the Rose-month was this sweet Rose taken.
For the Rose-kind hath she earth forsaken.
The Princess is the Rose, that here no longer blows.
From the stem by death's hand rudely shaken.
Then rest in the Rose-house.
Little Princess-Rosebud dear!
There life's Rose shall bloom again
In Heaven's sunshine clear.

While March struggled to get this into English words, two German ladies, who had made themselves of his party, passed reverently away and left him to pay the sacristan alone.

"That is all right," he said, when he came out. "I think we got the most value; and they didn't look as if they could afford it so well; though you never can tell, here. These ladies may be the highest kind of highhotes practising a praiseworthy economy. I hope the lesson won't be lost on us. They have saved enough by us for their coffee at the Orangery. Let us go and have a little willow-leaf tea!"

The Orangery perpetually lured them by what it had kept of the days when an Orangery was essential to the self-respect of every sovereign prince, and of so many private gentlemen. On their way they always passed the statue of Count Platen, the dull poet whom Heine's hate would have delivered so cruelly over to an immortality of contempt, but who stands there near the Schloss in a grass-plot prettily planted with flowers, and ignores his brilliant enemy in the comfortable durability of bronze; and there always awaited them in the old pleasaunce the pathos of Kaspar Hauser's fate; which his murder affixes to it with a red stain.

After their cups of willow leaves at the cafe they went up into that nook of the plantation where the simple shaft of church-warden's Gothic commemorates the assassination on the spot where it befell. Here the hapless youth, whose mystery will never be fathomed on earth, used to come for a little respite from his harsh guardian in Ansbach, homesick for the kindness of his Nuremberg friends; and here his murderer found him and dealt him the mortal blow.

March lingered upon the last sad circumstance of the tragedy in which the wounded boy dragged himself home, to suffer the suspicion and neglect of his guardian till death attested his good faith beyond cavil. He said this was the hardest thing to bear in all his story, and that he would like to have a look into the soul of the dull, unkind wretch who had so misread his charge. He was going on with an inquiry that pleased him much, when his wife pulled him abruptly away.

"Now, I see, you are yielding to the fascination of it, and you are wanting to take the material from Burnamy!"

"Oh, well, let him have the material; he will spoil it. And I can always reject it, if he offers it to 'Every Other Week'."

"I could believe, after your behavior to that poor woman about her son in Jersey City, you're really capable of it."

"What comprehensive inculpation! I had forgotten about that poor woman."

LI.

The letters which March had asked his Nuremberg banker to send them came just as they were leaving Ansbach. The landlord sent them down to the station, and Mrs. March opened them in the train, and read them first so that she could prepare him if there were anything annoying in them, as well as indulge her livelier curiosity.

"They're from both the children," she said, without waiting for him to ask. "You can look at them later. There's a very nice letter from Mrs. Adding to me, and one from dear little Rose for you." Then she hesitated, with her hand on a letter faced down in her lap. "And there's one from Agatha Triscoe, which I wonder what you'll think of." She delayed again, and then flashed it open before him, and waited with a sort of impassioned patience while he read it.

He read it, and gave it back to her. "There doesn't seem to be very much in it."

"That's it! Don't you think I had a right to there being something in it, after all I did for her?"

"I always hoped you hadn't done anything for her, but if you have, why should she give herself away on paper? It's a very proper letter."

"It's a little too proper, and it's the last I shall have to do with her. She knew that I should be on pins and needles till I heard how her father had taken Burnamy's being there, that night, and she doesn't say a word about it."

"The general may have had a tantrum that she couldn't describe. Perhaps she hasn't told him, yet."

"She would tell him instantly!" cried Mrs. March who began to find reason in the supposition, as well as comfort for the hurt which the girl's reticence had given her. "Or if she wouldn't, it would be because she was waiting for the best chance."

"That would be like the wise daughter of a difficult father. She may be waiting for the best chance to say how he took it. No, I'm all for Miss Triscoe, and I hope that now, if she's taken herself off our hands, she'll keep off."

"It's altogether likely that he's made her promise not to tell me anything about it," Mrs. March mused aloud.

"That would be unjust to a person who had behaved so discreetly as you have," said her husband.

They were on their way to Wurzburg, and at the first station, which was a junction, a lady mounted to their compartment just before the train began to move. She was stout and middle-aged, and had never been pretty, but she bore herself with a kind of authority in spite of her thread gloves, her dowdy gray travelling-dress, and a hat of lower middle-class English tastelessness. She took the only seat vacant, a backward-riding place beside a sleeping passenger who looked like a commercial traveller, but she seemed ill at ease in it, and March offered her his seat. She accepted it very promptly, and thanked him for it in the English of a German, and Mrs. March now classed her as a governess who had been teaching in England and had acquired the national feeling for dress. But in this character she found her interesting, and even a little pathetic, and she made her some overtures of talk which the other met eagerly enough. They were now running among low hills, not so picturesque as those between Eger and Nuremberg, but of much the same toylike quaintness in the villages dropped here and there in their valleys. One small town, completely walled, with its gray houses and red roofs, showed through the green of its trees and gardens so like a colored print in a child's story-book that Mrs. March cried out for joy in it, and then accounted for her rapture by explaining to the stranger that they were Americans and had never been in Germany before. The lady was not visibly affected by the fact, she said casually that she had often been in that little town, which she named; her uncle had a castle in the country back of it, and she came with her husband for the shooting in the autumn. By a natural transition she spoke of her children, for whom she had an English governess; she said she had never been in England, but had learnt the language from a governess in her own childhood; and through it all Mrs. March perceived that she was trying to impress them with her consequence. To humor her pose, she said they had been looking up the scene of Kaspar Hauser's death at Ansbach; and at this the stranger launched into such intimate particulars concerning him, and was so familiar at first hands with the facts of his life, that Mrs. March let her run on, too much amused with her pretensions to betray any doubt of her. She wondered if March were enjoying it all as much, and from time to time she tried to catch his eye, while the lady talked constantly and rather loudly, helping herself out with words from them both when her English failed her. In the safety of her perfect understanding of the case, Mrs. March now submitted farther, and even suffered some patronage from her, which in another mood she would have met with a decided snub.

As they drew in among the broad vine-webbed slopes of the Wurzburg, hills, the stranger said she was going to change there, and take a train on to Berlin. Mrs. March wondered whether she would be able to keep up the comedy to the last; and she had to own that she carried it off very easily when the friends whom she was expecting did not meet her on the arrival of their train. She refused March's offers of help, and remained quietly seated while he got out their wraps and bags. She returned with a hardy smile the cold leave Mrs. March took of her; and when a porter came to the door, and forced his way

by the Marches, to ask with anxious servility if she, were the Baroness von——
——, she bade the man get them. a 'traeger', and then come back for her. She
waved them a complacent adieu before they mixed with the crowd and lost
sight of her.

"Well, my dear," said March, addressing the snobbishness in his wife which
he knew to be so wholly impersonal, "you've mingled with one highhote,
anyway. I must say she didn't look it, any more than the Duke and Duchess
of Orleans, and yet she's only a baroness. Think of our being three hours in
the same compartment, and she doing all she could to impress us and our
getting no good of it! I hoped you were feeling her quality, so that we should
have it in the family, anyway, and always know what it was like. But so far,
the highhotes have all been terribly disappointing."

He teased on as they followed the traeger with their baggage out of the
station; and in the omnibus on the way to their hotel, he recurred to the loss
they had suffered in the baroness's failure to dramatize her nobility
effectually. "After all, perhaps she was as much disappointed in us. I don't
suppose we looked any more like democrats than she looked like an
aristocrat."

"But there's a great difference," Mrs. March returned at last. "It isn't at all a
parallel case. We were not real democrats, and she was a real aristocrat."

"To be sure. There is that way of looking at it. That's rather novel; I wish I
had thought of that myself. She was certainly more to blame than we were."

LII.

The square in front of the station was planted with flag-poles wreathed in evergreens; a triumphal arch was nearly finished, and a colossal allegory in imitation bronze was well on the way to completion, in honor of the majesties who were coming for the manoeuvres. The streets which the omnibus passed through to the Swan Inn were draped with the imperial German and the royal Bavarian colors; and the standards of the visiting nationalities decked the fronts of the houses where their military attaches were lodged; but the Marches failed to see our own banner, and were spared for the moment the ignominy of finding it over an apothecary shop in a retired avenue. The sun had come out, the sky overhead was of a smiling blue; and they felt the gala-day glow and thrill in the depths of their inextinguishable youth.

The Swan Inn sits on one of the long quays bordering the Main, and its windows look down upon the bridges and shipping of the river; but the traveller reaches it by a door in the rear, through an archway into a back street, where an odor dating back to the foundation of the city is waiting to welcome him.

The landlord was there, too, and he greeted the Marches so cordially that they fully partook his grief in being able to offer them rooms on the front of the house for two nights only. They reconciled themselves to the necessity of then turning out for the staff of the King of Saxony, the more readily because they knew that there was no hope of better things at any other hotel.

The rooms which they could have for the time were charming, and they came down to supper in a glazed gallery looking out on the river picturesque with craft of all fashions: with row-boats, sail-boats, and little steamers, but mainly with long black barges built up into houses in the middle, and defended each by a little nervous German dog. Long rafts of logs weltered in the sunset red which painted the swift current, and mantled the immeasurable vineyards of the hills around like the color of their ripening grapes. Directly in face rose a castled steep, which kept the ranging walls and the bastions and battlements of the time when such a stronghold could have defended the city from foes without or from tumult within. The arches of a stately bridge spanned the river sunsetward, and lifted a succession of colossal figures against the crimson sky.

"I guess we have been wasting our time, my dear," said March, as they, turned from this beauty to the question of supper. "I wish we had always been here!"

Their waiter had put them at a table in a division of the gallery beyond that which they entered, where some groups of officers were noisily supping. There was no one in their room but a man whose face was indistinguishable against the light, and two young girls who glanced at them with looks at once quelled and defiant, and then after a stare at the officers in the gallery beyond, whispered together with suppressed giggling. The man fed on without noticing them, except now and then to utter a growl that silenced the whispering and giggling for a moment. The Marches, from no positive evidence of any sense, decided that they were Americans.

"I don't know that I feel responsible for them as their fellow-countryman; I should, once," he said.

"It isn't that. It's the worry of trying to make out why they are just what they are," his wife returned.

The girls drew the man's attention to them and he looked at them for the first time; then after a sort of hesitation he went on with his supper. They had only begun theirs when he rose with the two girls, whom Mrs. March now saw to be of the same size and dressed alike, and came heavily toward them.

"I thought you was in Carlsbad," he said bluntly to March, with a nod at Mrs. March. He added, with a twist of his head toward the two girls, "My daughters," and then left them to her, while he talked on with her husband. "Come to see this foolery, I suppose. I'm on my way to the woods for my after-cure; but I thought I might as well stop and give the girls a chance; they got a week's vacation, anyway." Stoller glanced at them with a sort of troubled tenderness in his strong dull face.

"Oh, yes. I understood they were at school here," said March, and he heard one of them saying, in a sweet, high pipe to his wife:

"Ain't it just splendid? I ha'n't seen anything equal to it since the Worrld's Fairr." She spoke with a strong contortion of the Western r, and her sister hastened to put in:

"I don't think it's to be compared with the Worrld's Fairr. But these German girls, here, just think it's great. It just does me good to laff at 'em, about it. I like to tell 'em about the electric fountain and the Courrt of Iionorr when they get to talkin' about the illuminations they're goun' to have. You goun' out to the parade? You better engage your carriage right away if you arre. The carrs'll be a perfect jam. Father's engaged ourrs; he had to pay sixty marrks forr it."

They chattered on without shyness and on as easy terms with a woman of three times their years as if she had been a girl of their own age; they willingly took the whole talk to themselves, and had left her quite outside of it before Stoller turned to her.

"I been telling Mr. March here that you better both come to the parade with us. I guess my twospanner will hold five; or if it won't, we'll make it. I don't believe there's a carriage left in Wurzburg; and if you go in the cars, you'll have to walk three or four miles before you get to the parade-ground. You think it over," he said to March. "Nobody else is going to have the places, anyway, and you can say yes at the last minute just as well as now."

He moved off with his girls, who looked over their shoulders at the officers as they passed on through the adjoining room.

"My dear!" cried Mrs. March. "Didn't you suppose he classed us with Burnamy in that business? Why should he be polite to us?"

"Perhaps he wants you to chaperon his daughters. He's probably heard of your performance at the Kurhaus ball. But he knows that I thought Burnamy in the wrong. This may be Stoller's way of wiping out an obligation. Wouldn't you like to go with him?"

"The mere thought of his being in the same town is prostrating. I'd far rather he hated us; then he would avoid us."

"Well, he doesn't own the town, and if it comes to the worst, perhaps we can avoid him. Let us go out, anyway, and see if we can't."

"No, no; I'm too tired; but you go. And get all the maps and guides you can; there's so very little in Baedeker, and almost nothing in that great hulking Bradshaw of yours; and I'm sure there must be the most interesting history of Wurzburg. Isn't it strange that we haven't the slightest association with the name?"

"I've been rummaging in my mind, and I've got hold of an association at last," said March. "It's beer; a sign in a Sixth Avenue saloon window Wurzburger Hof-Brau."

"No matter if it is beer. Find some sketch of the history, and we'll try to get away from the Stollers in it. I pitied those wild girls, too. What crazy images of the world must fill their empty minds! How their ignorant thoughts must go whirling out into the unknown! I don't envy their father. Do hurry back! I shall be thinking about them every instant till you come."

She said this, but in their own rooms it was so soothing to sit looking through the long twilight at the lovely landscape that the sort of bruise given by their encounter with the Stollers had left her consciousness before March returned. She made him admire first the convent church on a hill further up the river which exactly balanced the fortress in front of them, and then she seized upon the little books he had brought, and set him to exploring the labyrinths of their German, with a mounting exultation in his discoveries. There was a general guide to the city, and a special guide, with plans and personal details of the approaching manoeuvres and the princes who were to figure in them; and there was a sketch of the local history: a kind of thing that the Germans know how to write particularly, well, with little gleams of pleasant humor blinking through it. For the study of this, Mrs. March realized, more and more passionately, that they were in the very most central and convenient point, for the history of Wurzburg might be said to have begun with her prince-bishops, whose rule had begun in the twelfth century, and who had built, on a forgotten Roman work, the fortress of the Marienburg on that vineyarded hill over against the Swan Inn. There had of course been history before that, but 'nothing so clear, nothing so peculiarly swell, nothing that so united the glory of this world and the next as that of the prince-bishops. They had made the Marienburg their home, and kept it against foreign and domestic foes for five hundred years. Shut within its well-armed walls they had awed the often-turbulent city across the Main; they had held it against the embattled farmers in the Peasants' War, and had splendidly lost it to Gustavus Adolphus, and then got it back again and held it till Napoleon took it from them. He gave it with their flock to the Bavarians, who in turn briefly yielded it to the Prussians in 1866, and were now in apparently final possession of it.

Before the prince-bishops, Charlemagne and Barbarossa had come and gone, and since the prince-bishops there had been visiting thrones and kingdoms enough in the ancient city, which was soon to be illustrated by the presence of imperial Germany, royal, Wirtemberg and Saxony, grand-ducal Baden and Weimar, and a surfeit of all the minor potentates among those who speak the beautiful language of the Ja.

But none of these could dislodge the prince-bishops from that supreme place which they had at once taken in Mrs. March's fancy. The potentates were all going to be housed in the vast palace which the prince-bishops had built themselves in Wurzburg as soon as they found it safe to come down from their stronghold of Marienburg, and begin to adorn their city, and to confirm it in its intense fidelity to the Church. Tiepolo had come up out of Italy to fresco their palace, where he wrought year after year, in that worldly taste which has somehow come to express the most sovereign moment of ecclesiasticism. It prevailed so universally in Wurzburg that it left her with the name of the Rococo City, intrenched in a period of time equally remote from early Christianity and modern Protestantism. Out of her sixty thousand souls, only ten thousand are now of the reformed religion, and these bear about the same relation to the Catholic spirit of the place that the Gothic architecture bears to the baroque.

As long as the prince-bishops lasted the Wurzburgers got on very well with but one newspaper, and perhaps the smallest amount of merrymaking known outside of the colony of Massachusetts Bay at the same epoch. The prince-bishops had their finger in everybody's pie, and they portioned out the cakes and ale, which were made according to formulas of their own. The distractions were all of a religious character; churches, convents, monasteries, abounded; ecclesiastical processions and solemnities were the spectacles that edified if they did not amuse the devout population.

It seemed to March an ironical outcome of all this spiritual severity that one of the greatest modern scientific discoveries should have been made in Wurzburg, and that the Roentgen rays should now be giving her name a splendor destined to eclipse the glories of her past.

Mrs. March could not allow that they would do so; or at least that the name of Roentgen would ever lend more lustre to his city than that of Longfellow's Walther von der Vogelweide. She was no less surprised than pleased to realize that this friend of the birds was a Wurzburger, and she said that their first pilgrimage in the morning should be to the church where he lies buried.

LIII.

March went down to breakfast not quite so early as his wife had planned, and left her to have her coffee in her room. He got a pleasant table in the gallery overlooking the river, and he decided that the landscape, though it now seemed to be rather too much studied from a drop-certain, had certainly lost nothing of its charm in the clear morning light. The waiter brought his breakfast, and after a little delay came back with a card which he insisted was for March. It was not till he put on his glasses and read the name of Mr. R. M. Kenby that he was able at all to agree with the waiter, who stood passive at his elbow.

"Well," he said, "why wasn't this card sent up last night?"

The waiter explained that the gentleman had just, given him his card, after asking March's nationality, and was then breakfasting in the next room. March caught up his napkin and ran round the partition wall, and Kenby rose with his napkin and hurried to meet him.

"I thought it must be you," he called out, joyfully, as they struck their extended hands together, "but so many people look alike, nowadays, that I don't trust my eyes any more."

Kenby said he had spent the time since they last met partly in Leipsic and partly in Gotha, where he had amused himself in rubbing up his rusty German. As soon as he realized that Wurzburg was so near he had slipped down from Gotha for a glimpse of the manoeuvres. He added that he supposed March was there to see them, and he asked with a quite unembarrassed smile if they had met Mr. Adding in Carlsbad, and without heeding March's answer, he laughed and added: "Of course, I know she must have told Mrs. March all about it."

March could not deny this; he laughed, too; though in his wife's absence he felt bound to forbid himself anything more explicit.

"I don't give it up, you know," Kenby went on, with perfect case. "I'm not a young fellow, if you call thirty-nine old."

"At my age I don't," March put in, and they roared together, in men's security from the encroachments of time.

"But she happens to be the only woman I've ever really wanted to marry, for more than a few days at a stretch. You know how it is with us."

"Oh, yes, I know," said March, and they shouted again.

"We're in love, and we're out of love, twenty times. But this isn't a mere fancy; it's a conviction. And there's no reason why she shouldn't marry me."

March smiled gravely, and his smile was not lost upon Kenby. "You mean the boy," he said. "Well, I like Rose," and now March really felt swept from his feet. "She doesn't deny that she likes me, but she seems to think that her marrying again will take her from him; the fact is, it will only give me to him. As for devoting her whole life to him, she couldn't do a worse thing for him. What the boy needs is a man's care, and a man's will—Good heavens! You don't think I could ever be unkind to the little soul?" Kenby threw himself forward over the table.

"My dear fellow!" March protested.

"I'd rather cut off my right hand!" Kenby pursued, excitedly, and then he said, with a humorous drop: "The fact is, I don't believe I should want her so much if I couldn't have Rose too. I want to have them both. So far, I've only got no for an answer; but I'm not going to keep it. I had a letter from Rose at Carlsbad, the other day; and—"

The waiter came forward with a folded scrap of paper on his salver, which March knew must be from his wife. "What is keeping you so?" she wrote. "I am all ready." "It's from Mrs. March," he explained to Kenby. "I am going out with her on some errands. I'm awfully glad to see you again. We must talk it all over, and you must—you mustn't—Mrs. March will want to see you later—I—Are you in the hotel?"

"Oh yes. I'll see you at the one-o'clock table d'hote, I suppose."

March went away with his head whirling in the question whether he should tell his wife at once of Kenby's presence, or leave her free for the pleasures of Wurzburg, till he could shape the fact into some safe and acceptable form. She met him at the door with her guide-books, wraps and umbrellas, and would hardly give him time to get on his hat and coat.

"Now, I want you to avoid the Stollers as far as you can see them. This is to be a real wedding-journey day, with no extraneous acquaintance to bother; the more strangers the better. Wurzburg is richer than anything I imagined. I've looked it all up; I've got the plan of the city, so that we can easily find the way. We'll walk first, and take carriages whenever we get tired. We'll go to the cathedral at once; I want a good gulp of rococo to begin with; there wasn't half enough of it at Ansbach. Isn't it strange how we've come round to it?"

She referred to that passion for the Gothic which they had obediently imbibed from Ruskin in the days of their early Italian travel and courtship, when all the English-speaking world bowed down to him in devout aversion from the renaissance, and pious abhorrence of the rococo.

"What biddable little things we were!" she went on, while March was struggling to keep Kenby in the background of his consciousness. "The rococo must have always had a sneaking charm for us, when we were pinning our faith to pointed arches; and yet I suppose we were perfectly sincere. Oh, look at that divinely ridiculous Madonna!" They were now making their way out of the crooked footway behind their hotel toward the street leading to the cathedral, and she pointed to the Blessed Virgin over the door of some religious house, her drapery billowing about her feet; her body twisting to show the sculptor's mastery of anatomy, and the halo held on her tossing head with the help of stout gilt rays. In fact, the Virgin's whole figure was gilded, and so was that of the child in her arms. "Isn't she delightful?"

"I see what you mean," said March, with a dubious glance at the statue, "but I'm not sure, now, that I wouldn't like something quieter in my Madonnas."

The thoroughfare which they emerged upon, with the cathedral ending the prospective, was full of the holiday so near at hand. The narrow sidewalks were thronged with people, both soldiers and civilians, and up the middle of the street detachments of military came and went, halting the little horse-cars and the huge beer-wagons which otherwise seemed to have the sole right to the streets of Wurzburg; they came jingling or thundering out of the aide streets and hurled themselves round the corners reckless of the passers, who escaped alive by flattening themselves like posters against the house walls. There were peasants, men and women, in the costume which the unbroken course of their country life had kept as quaint as it was a hundred years before; there were citizens in the misfits of the latest German fashions; there were soldiers of all arms in their vivid uniforms, and from time to time there were pretty young girls in white dresses with low necks, and bare arms gloved to the elbows, who were following a holiday custom of the place in going about the streets in ball costume. The shop windows were filled with portraits of the Emperor and the Empress, and the Prince-Regent and the ladies of his family; the German and Bavarian colors draped the facades of the houses and festooned the fantastic Madonnas posing above so many portals. The modern patriotism included the ancient piety without disturbing it; the rococo city remained ecclesiastical through its new imperialism, and kept the stamp given it by the long rule of the prince-bishops under the sovereignty of its King and the suzerainty of its Kaiser.

The Marches escaped from the present, when they entered the cathedral, as wholly as if they had taken hold of the horns of the altar, though they were far from literally doing this in an interior so grandiose. There area few rococo churches in Italy, and perhaps more in Spain, which approach the perfection achieved by the Wurzburg cathedral in the baroque style. For once one sees what that style can do in architecture and sculpture, and whatever one may say of the details, one cannot deny that there is a prodigiously effective keeping in it all. This interior came together, as the decorators say, with a harmony that the travellers had felt nowhere in their earlier experience of the rococo. It was, unimpeachably perfect in its way, "Just," March murmured to his wife, "as the social and political and scientific scheme of the eighteenth century was perfected in certain times and places. But the odd thing is to find the apotheosis of the rococo away up here in Germany. I wonder how much the prince-bishops really liked it. But they had become rococo, too! Look at that row of their statues on both sides of the nave! What magnificent swell! How they abash this poor plain Christ, here; he would like to get behind the pillar; he knows that he could never lend himself to the baroque style. It expresses the eighteenth century, though. But how you long for some little hint of the thirteenth, or even the nineteenth."

"I don't," she whispered back. "I'm perfectly wild with Wurzburg. I like to have a thing go as far as it can. At Nuremberg I wanted all the Gothic I could get, and in Wurzburg I want all the baroque I can get. I am consistent."

She kept on praising herself to his disadvantage, as women do, all the way to the Neumunster Church, where they were going to revere the tomb of Walther von der Vogelweide, not so much for his own sake as for Longfellow's. The older poet lies buried within, but his monument is outside the church, perhaps for the greater convenience of the sparrows, which now represent the birds he loved. The cenotaph is surmounted by a broad vase, and around this are thickly perched the effigies of the Meistersinger's feathered friends, from whom the canons of the church, as Mrs. March read aloud from her Baedeker, long ago directed his bequest to themselves. In revenge for their lawless greed the defrauded beneficiaries choose to burlesque the affair by looking like the four-and-twenty blackbirds when the pie was opened.

She consented to go for a moment to the Gothic Marienkapelle with her husband in the revival of his mediaeval taste, and she was rewarded amidst its thirteenth-century sincerity by his recantation. "You are right! Baroque is the thing for Wurzburg; one can't enjoy Gothic here any more than one could enjoy baroque in Nuremberg."

Reconciled in the rococo, they now called a carriage, and went to visit the palace of the prince-bishops who had so well known how to make the heavenly take the image and superscription of the worldly; and they were jointly indignant to find it shut against the public in preparation for the imperialities and royalties coming to occupy it. They were in time for the noon guard-mounting, however, and Mrs. March said that the way the retiring squad kicked their legs out in the high martial step of the German soldiers was a perfect expression of the insolent militarism of their empire, and was of itself enough to make one thank Heaven that one was an

American and a republican. She softened a little toward their system when it proved that the garden of the palace was still open, and yet more when she sank down upon a bench between two marble groups representing the Rape of Proserpine and the Rape of Europa. They stood each in a gravelled plot, thickly overrun by a growth of ivy, and the vine climbed the white naked limbs of the nymphs, who were present on a pretence of gathering flowers, but really to pose at the spectators, and clad them to the waist and shoulders with an effect of modesty never meant by the sculptor, but not displeasing. There was an old fountain near, its stone rim and centre of rock-work green with immemorial mould, and its basin quivering between its water-plants under the soft fall of spray. At a waft of fitful breeze some leaves of early autumn fell from the trees overhead upon the elderly pair where they sat, and a little company of sparrows came and hopped about their feet. Though the square without was so all astir with festive expectation, there were few people in the garden; three or four peasant women in densely fluted white skirts and red aprons and shawls wandered by and stared at the Europa and at the Proserpine.

It was a precious moment in which the charm of the city's past seemed to culminate, and they were loath to break it by speech.

"Why didn't we have something like all this on our first wedding journey?" she sighed at last. "To think of our battening from Boston to Niagara and back! And how hard we tried to make something of Rochester and Buffalo, of Montreal and Quebec!"

"Niagara wasn't so bad," he said, "and I will never go back on Quebec."

"Ah, but if we could have had Hamburg and Leipsic, and Carlsbad and Nuremberg, and Ansbach and Wurzburg! Perhaps this is meant as a compensation for our lost youth. But I can't enjoy it as I could when I was young. It's wasted on my sere and yellow leaf. I wish Burnamy and Miss Triscoe were here; I should like to try this garden on them."

"They wouldn't care for it," he replied, and upon a daring impulse he added, "Kenby and Mrs. Adding might." If she took this suggestion in good part, he could tell her that Kenby was in Wurzburg.

"Don't speak of them! They're in just that besotted early middle-age when life has settled into a self-satisfied present, with no past and no future; the most philistine, the most bourgeois, moment of existence. Better be elderly at once, as far as appreciation of all this goes." She rose and put her hand on his arm, and pushed him away in the impulsive fashion of her youth, across alleys of old trees toward a balustraded terrace in the background which had tempted her.

"It isn't so bad, being elderly," he said. "By that time we have accumulated enough past to sit down and really enjoy its associations. We have got all sorts of perspectives and points of view. We know where we are at."

"I don't mind being elderly. The world's just as amusing as ever, and lots of disagreeable things have dropped out. It's the getting more than elderly; it's the getting old; and then—"

They shrank a little closer together, and walked on in silence till he said, "Perhaps there's something else, something better—somewhere."

They had reached the balustraded terrace, and were pausing for pleasure in the garden tops below, with the flowery spaces, and the statued fountains all coming together. She put her hand on one of the fat little urchin-groups on the stone coping. "I don't want cherubs, when I can have these putti. And those old prince-bishops didn't, either!"

"I don't suppose they kept a New England conscience," he said, with a vague smile. "It would be difficult in the presence of the rococo."

They left the garden through the beautiful gate which the old court ironsmith Oegg hammered out in lovely forms of leaves and flowers, and shaped laterally upward, as lightly as if with a waft of his hand, in gracious Louis Quinze curves; and they looked back at it in the kind of despair which any perfection inspires. They said how feminine it was, how exotic, how expressive of a luxurious ideal of life which art had purified and left eternally charming. They remembered their Ruskinian youth, and the confidence with which they would once have condemned it; and they had a sense of recreance in now admiring it; but they certainly admired it, and it remained for them the supreme expression of that time-soul, mundane, courtly, aristocratic, flattering, which once influenced the art of the whole world, and which had here so curiously found its apotheosis in a city remote from its native place and under a rule sacerdotally vowed to austerity. The vast superb palace of the prince bishops, which was now to house a whole troop of sovereigns, imperial, royal, grand ducal and ducal, swelled aloft in superb amplitude; but it did not realize their historic pride so effectively as this exquisite work of the court ironsmith. It related itself in its aerial beauty to that of the Tiepolo frescoes which the travellers knew were swimming and soaring on the ceilings within, and from which it seemed to accent their exclusion with a delicate irony, March said. "Or iron-mongery," he corrected himself upon reflection.

LIV.

He had forgotten Kenby in these aesthetic interests, but he remembered him again when he called a carriage, and ordered it driven to their hotel. It was the hour of the German mid-day table d'hote, and they would be sure to meet him there. The question now was how March should own his presence in time to prevent his wife from showing her ignorance of it to Kenby himself, and he was still turning the question hopelessly over in his mind when the sight of the hotel seemed to remind her of a fact which she announced.

"Now, my dear, I am tired to death, and I am not going to sit through a long table d'hote. I want you to send me up a simple beefsteak and a cup of tea to our rooms; and I don't want you to come near for hours; because I intend to take a whole afternoon nap. You can keep all the maps and plans, and guides, and you had better go and see what the Volksfest is like; it will give you some notion of the part the people are really taking in all this official celebration, and you know I don't care. Don't come up after dinner to see how I am getting along; I shall get along; and if you should happen to wake me after I had dropped off—"

Kenby had seen them arrive from where he sat at the reading-room window, waiting for the dinner hour, and had meant to rush out and greet Mrs. March as they passed up the corridor. But she looked so tired that he had decided to spare her till she came down to dinner; and as he sat with March at their soup, he asked if she were not well.

March explained, and he provisionally invented some regrets from her that she should not see Kenby till supper.

Kenby ordered a bottle of one of the famous Wurzburg wines for their mutual consolation in her absence, and in the friendliness which its promoted they agreed to spend the afternoon together. No man is so inveterate a husband as not to take kindly an occasional release to bachelor companionship, and before the dinner was over they agreed that they would go to the Volksfest, and get some notion of the popular life and amusements of Wurzburg, which was one of the few places where Kenby had never been before; and they agreed that they would walk.

Their way was partly up the quay of the Main, past a barrack full of soldiers. They met detachments of soldiers everywhere, infantry, artillery, cavalry.

"This is going to be a great show," Kenby said, meaning the manoeuvres, and he added, as if now he had kept away from the subject long enough and had a right to recur to it, at least indirectly, "I should like to have Rose see it, and get his impressions."

"I've an idea he wouldn't approve of it. His mother says his mind is turning more and more to philanthropy."

Kenby could not forego such a chance to speak of Mrs. Adding. "It's one of the prettiest things to see how she understands Rose. It's charming to see them together. She wouldn't have half the attraction without him."

"Oh, yes," March assented. He had often wondered how a man wishing to marry a widow managed with the idea of her children by another marriage; but if Kenby was honest; it was much simpler than he had supposed. He could not say this to him, however, and in a certain embarrassment he had with the conjecture in his presence he attempted a diversion. "We're promised something at the Volksfest which will be a great novelty to us as Americans. Our driver told us this morning that one of the houses there was built entirely of wood."

When they reached the grounds of the Volksfest, this civil feature of the great military event at hand, which the Marches had found largely set forth in the programme of the parade, did not fully keep the glowing promises made for it; in fact it could not easily have done so. It was in a pleasant neighborhood of new villas such as form the modern quarter of every German city, and the Volksfest was even more unfinished than its environment. It was not yet enclosed by the fence which was to hide its wonders from the non-paying public, but March and Kenby went in through an archway where the gate-money was as effectually collected from them as if they were barred every other entrance.

The wooden building was easily distinguishable from the other edifices because these were tents and booths still less substantial. They did not make out its function, but of the others four sheltered merry-go-rounds, four were beer-gardens, four were restaurants, and the rest were devoted to amusements of the usual country-fair type. Apparently they had little attraction for country people. The Americans met few peasants in the grounds, and neither at the Edison kinematograph, where they refreshed their patriotism with some scenes of their native life, nor at the little theatre where they saw the sports of the arena revived, in the wrestle of a woman with a bear, did any of the people except tradesmen and artisans seem to be taking part in the festival expression of the popular pleasure.

The woman, who finally threw the bear, whether by slight, or by main strength, or by a previous understanding with him, was a slender creature, pathetically small and not altogether plain; and March as they walked away lapsed into a pensive muse upon her strange employ. He wondered how she came to take it up, and whether she began with the bear when they were both very young, and she could easily throw him.

"Well, women have a great deal more strength than we suppose," Kenby began with a philosophical air that gave March the hope of some rational conversation. Then his eye glazed with a far-off look, and a doting smile came into his face. "When we went through the Dresden gallery together, Rose and I were perfectly used up at the end of an hour, but his mother kept on as long as there was anything to see, and came away as fresh as a peach."

Then March saw that it was useless to expect anything different from him, and he let him talk on about Mrs. Adding all the rest of the way back to the hotel. Kenby seemed only to have begun when they reached the door, and wanted to continue the subject in the reading-room.

March pleaded his wish to find how his wife had got through the afternoon, and he escaped to her. He would have told her now that Kenby was in the house, but he was really so sick of the fact himself that he could not speak of it at once, and he let her go on celebrating all she had seen from the window since she had waked from her long nap. She said she could never be glad enough that they had come just at that time. Soldiers had been going by the whole afternoon, and that made it so feudal.

"Yes," he assented. "But aren't you coming up to the station with me to see the Prince-Regent arrive? He's due at seven, you know."

"I declare I had forgotten all about it. No, I'm not equal to it. You must go; you can tell me everything; be sure to notice how the Princess Maria looks; the last of the Stuarts, you know; and some people consider her the rightful Queen of England; and I'll have the supper ordered, and we can go down as soon as you've got back."

LV.

March felt rather shabby stealing away without Kenby; but he had really had as much of Mrs. Adding as he could stand, for one day, and he was even beginning to get sick of Rose. Besides, he had not sent back a line for 'Every Other Week' yet, and he had made up his mind to write a sketch of the manoeuvres. To this end he wished to receive an impression of the Prince-Regent's arrival which should not be blurred or clouded by other interests. His wife knew the kind of thing he liked to see, and would have helped him out with his observations, but Kenby would have got in the way, and would have clogged the movement of his fancy in assigning the facts to the parts he would like them to play in the sketch.

At least he made some such excuses to himself as he hurried along toward the Kaiserstrasse. The draught of universal interest in that direction had left the other streets almost deserted, but as he approached the thoroughfare he found all the ways blocked, and the horse-cars, ordinarily so furiously headlong, arrested by the multiple ranks of spectators on the sidewalks. The avenue leading from the railway station to the palace was decorated with flags and garlands, and planted with the stems of young firs and birches. The doorways were crowded, and the windows dense with eager faces peering out of the draped bunting. The carriageway was kept clear by mild policemen who now and then allowed one of the crowd to cross it.

The crowd was made up mostly of women and boys, and when March joined them, they had already been waiting an hour for the sight of the princes who were to bless them with a vision of the faery race which kings always are to common men. He thought the people looked dull, and therefore able to bear the strain of expectation with patience better than a livelier race. They relieved it by no attempt at joking; here and there a dim smile dawned on a weary face, but it seemed an effect of amiability rather than humor. There was so little of this, or else it was so well bridled by the solemnity of the occasion, that not a man, woman, or child laughed when a bareheaded maid-servant broke through the lines and ran down between them with a life-size plaster bust of the Emperor William in her arms: she carried it like an overgrown infant, and in alarm at her conspicuous part she cast frightened looks from side to side without arousing any sort of notice. Undeterred by her failure, a young dog, parted from his owner, and seeking him in the crowd, pursued his search in a wild flight down the guarded roadway with an air of anxiety that in America would have won him thunders of applause, and all sorts of kindly encouragements to greater speed. But this German crowd witnessed his progress apparently without interest, and without a sign of pleasure. They were there to see the Prince-Regent arrive, and they did not suffer themselves to be distracted by any preliminary excitement. Suddenly the indefinable emotion which expresses the fulfilment of expectation in a waiting crowd passed through the multitude, and before he realized it March was looking into the friendly gray-bearded face of the Prince-Regent, for the moment that his carriage allowed in passing. This came first preceded by four outriders, and followed by other simple equipages of Bavarian blue, full of highnesses of all grades. Beside the Regent sat his daughter-in-law, the Princess Maria, her silvered hair framing a face as plain and good as the Regent's, if not so intelligent.

He, in virtue of having been born in Wurzburg, is officially supposed to be specially beloved by his fellow townsmen; and they now testified their affection as he whirled through their ranks, bowing right and left, by what passes in Germany for a cheer. It is the word Hoch, groaned forth from abdominal depths, and dismally prolonged in a hollow roar like that which the mob makes behind the scenes at the theatre before bursting in visible tumult on the stage. Then the crowd dispersed, and March came away wondering why such a kindly-looking Prince-Regent should not have given them a little longer sight of himself; after they had waited so patiently for hours to see him. But doubtless in those countries, he concluded, the art of keeping the sovereign precious by suffering him to be rarely and briefly seen is wisely studied.

On his way home he resolved to confess Kenby's presence; and he did so as soon as he sat down to supper with his wife. "I ought to have told you the first thing after breakfast. But when I found you in that mood of having the place all to ourselves, I put it off."

"You took terrible chances, my dear," she said, gravely.

"And I have been terribly punished. You've no idea how much Kenby has talked to me about Mrs. Adding!"

She broke out laughing. "Well, perhaps you've suffered enough. But you can see now, can't you, that it would have been awful if I had met him, and let out that I didn't know he was here?"

"Terrible. But if I had told, it would have spoiled the whole morning for you; you couldn't have thought of anything else."

"Oh, I don't know," she said, airily. "What should you think if I told you I had known he was here ever since last night?" She went on in delight at the start he gave. "I saw him come into the hotel while you were gone for the guide-books, and I determined to keep it from you as long as I could; I knew it would worry you. We've both been very nice; and I forgive you," she hurried on, "because I've really got something to tell you."

"Don't tell me that Burnamy is here!"

"Don't jump to conclusions! No, Burnamy isn't here, poor fellow! And don't suppose that I'm guilty of concealment because I haven't told you before. I was just thinking whether I wouldn't spare you till morning, but now I shall let you take the brunt of it. Mrs. Adding and Rose are here." She gave the fact time to sink in, and then she added, "And Miss Triscoe and her father are here."

"What is the matter with Major Eltwin and his wife being here, too? Are they in our hotel?"

"No, they are not. They came to look for rooms while you were off waiting for the Prince-Regent, and I saw them. They intended to go to Frankfort for the manoeuvres, but they heard that there was not even standing-room there, and so the general telegraphed to the Spanischer Hof, and they all came here. As it is, he will have to room with Rose, and Agatha and Mrs. Adding will room together. I didn't think Agatha was looking very well; she looked unhappy; I don't believe she's heard, from Burnamy yet; I hadn't a chance to ask her. And there's something else that I'm afraid will fairly make you sick."

"Oh, no; go on. I don't think anything can do that, after an afternoon of Kenby's confidences."

"It's worse than Kenby," she said with a sigh. "You know I told you at Carlsbad I thought that ridiculous old thing was making up to Mrs. Adding."

"Kenby? Why of co—"

"Don't be stupid, my dear! No, not Kenby: General Triscoe. I wish you could have been here to see him paying her all sort; of silly attentions, and hear him making her compliments."

"Thank you. I think I'm just as well without it. Did she pay him silly attentions and compliments, too?"

"That's the only thing that can make me forgive her for his wanting her. She was keeping him at arm's-length the whole time, and she was doing it so as not to make him contemptible before his daughter."

"It must have been hard. And Rose?"

"Rose didn't seem very well. He looks thin and pale; but he's sweeter than ever. She's certainly commoner clay than Rose. No, I won't say that! It's really nothing but General Triscoe's being an old goose about her that makes her seem so, and it isn't fair."

March went down to his coffee in the morning with the delicate duty of telling Kenby that Mrs. Adding was in town. Kenby seemed to think it quite natural she should wish to see the manoeuvres, and not at all strange that she should come to them with General Triscoe and his daughter. He asked if March would not go with him to call upon her after breakfast, and as this was in the line of his own instructions from Mrs. March, he went.

They found Mrs. Adding with the Triscoes, and March saw nothing that was not merely friendly, or at the most fatherly, in the general's behavior toward her. If Mrs. Adding or Miss Triscoe saw more, they hid it in a guise of sisterly affection for each other. At the most the general showed a gayety which one would not have expected of him under any conditions, and which the fact that he and Rose had kept each other awake a good deal the night before seemed so little adapted to call out. He joked with Rose about their room and their beds, and put on a comradery with him that was not a perfect fit, and that suffered by contrast with the pleasure of the boy and Kenby in meeting. There was a certain question in the attitude of Mrs. Adding till March helped Kenby to account for his presence; then she relaxed in an effect of security so tacit that words overstate it, and began to make fun of Rose.

March could not find that Miss Triscoe looked unhappy, as his wife had said; he thought simply that she had grown plainer; but when he reported this, she lost her patience with him. In a girl, she said, plainness was unhappiness; and she wished to know when he would ever learn to look an inch below the surface: She was sure that Agatha Triscoe had not heard from Burnamy since the Emperor's birthday; that she was at swords'-points with her father, and so desperate that she did not care what became of her.

He had left Kenby with the others, and now, after his wife had talked herself tired of them all, he proposed going out again to look about the city, where there was nothing for the moment to remind them of the presence of their friends or even of their existence. She answered that she was worrying about all those people, and trying to work out their problem for them. He asked why she did not let them work it out themselves as they would have to do, after all her worry, and she said that where her sympathy had been excited she could not stop worrying, whether it did any good or not, and she could not respect any one who could drop things so completely out of his mind as he could; she had never been able to respect that in him.

"I know, my dear," he assented. "But I don't think it's a question of moral responsibility; it's a question of mental structure, isn't it? Your consciousness isn't built in thought-tight compartments, and one emotion goes all through it, and sinks you; but I simply close the doors and shut the emotion in, and keep on."

The fancy pleased him so much that he worked it out in all its implications, and could not, after their long experience of each other, realize that she was not enjoying the joke too, till she said she saw that he merely wished to tease.

Then, too late, he tried to share her worry; but she protested that she was not worrying at all; that she cared nothing about those people: that she was nervous, she was tired; and she wished he would leave her, and go out alone.

He found himself in the street again, and he perceived that he must be walking fast when a voice called him by name, and asked him what his hurry was. The voice was Stoller's, who got into step with him and followed the first with a second question.

"Made up your mind to go to the manoeuvres with me?"

His bluntness made it easy for March to answer: "I'm afraid my wife couldn't stand the drive back and forth."

"Come without her."

"Thank you. It's very kind of you. I'm not certain that I shall go at all. If I do, I shall run out by train, and take my chances with the crowd."

Stoller insisted no further. He felt no offence at the refusal of his offer, or chose to show none. He said, with the same uncouth abruptness as before: "Heard anything of that fellow since he left Carlsbad?"

"Burnamy?"

"Mm."

"No."

"Know where he is?"

"I don't in the least."

Stoller let another silence elapse while they hurried on, before he said, "I got to thinking what he done afterwards. He wasn't bound to look out for me; he might suppose I knew what I was about."

March turned his face and stared in Stoller's, which he was letting hang forward as he stamped heavily on. Had the disaster proved less than he had feared, and did he still want Burnamy's help in patching up the broken pieces; or did he really wish to do Burnamy justice to his friend?

In any case March's duty was clear. "I think Burnamy was bound to look out for you; Mr. Stoller, and I am glad to know that he saw it in the same light."

"I know he did," said Stoker with a blaze as from a long-smouldering fury, "and damn him, I'm not going to have it. I'm not going to, plead the baby act with him, or with any man. You tell him so, when you get the chance. You tell him I don't hold him accountable for anything I made him do. That ain't business; I don't want him around me, any more; but if he wants to go back to the paper he can have his place. You tell him I stand by what I done; and it's all right between him and me. I hain't done anything about it, the way I wanted him to help me to; I've let it lay, and I'm a-going to. I guess it ain't going to do me any harm, after all; our people hain't got very long memories; but if it is, let it. You tell him it's all right."

"I don't know where he is, Mr. Stoller, and I don't know that I care to be the bearer of your message," said March.

"Why not?"

"Why, for one thing, I don't agree with you that it's all right. Your choosing to stand by the consequences of Burnamy's wrong doesn't undo it. As I understand, you don't pardon it—"

Stoller gulped and did not answer at once. Then he said, "I stand by what I done. I'm not going to let him say I turned him down for doing what I told him to, because I hadn't the sense to know what I was about."

"Ah, I don't think it's a thing he'll like to speak of in any case," said March.

Stoller left him, at the corner they had reached, as abruptly as he had joined him, and March hurried back to his wife, and told her what had just passed between him and Stoller.

She broke out, "Well, I am surprised at you, my dear! You have always accused me of suspecting people, and attributing bad motives; and here you've refused even to give the poor man the benefit of the doubt. He merely wanted to save his savage pride with you, and that's all he wants to do with Burnamy. How could it hurt the poor boy to know that Stoller doesn't blame him? Why should you refuse to give his message to Burnamy? I don't want you to ridicule me for my conscience any more, Basil; you're twice as bad as I ever was. Don't you think that a person can ever expiate an offence? I've often heard you say that if any one owned his fault, he put it from him, and it was the same as if it hadn't been; and hasn't Burnamy owned up over and over again? I'm astonished at you, dearest."

March was in fact somewhat astonished at himself in the light of her reasoning; but she went on with some sophistries that restored him to his self-righteousness.

"I suppose you think he has interfered with Stoller's political ambition, and injured him in that way. Well, what if he has? Would it be a good thing to have a man like that succeed in politics? You're always saying that the low character of our politicians is the ruin of the country; and I'm sure," she added, with a prodigious leap over all the sequences, "that Mr. Stoller is acting nobly; and it's your duty to help him relieve Burnamy's mind." At the laugh he broke into she hastened to say, "Or if you won't, I hope you'll not object to my doing so, for I shall, anyway!"

She rose as if she were going to begin at once, in spite of his laughing; and in fact she had already a plan for coming to Stoller's assistance by getting at Burnamy through Miss Triscoe, whom she suspected of knowing where he was. There had been no chance for them to speak of him either that morning or the evening before, and after a great deal of controversy with herself in her husband's presence she decided to wait till they came naturally together the next morning for the walk to the Capuchin Church on the hill beyond the river, which they had agreed to take. She could not keep from writing a note to Miss Triscoe begging her to be sure to come, and hinting that she had something very important to speak of.

She was not sure but she had been rather silly to do this, but when they met the girl confessed that she had thought of giving up the walk, and might not have come except for Mrs. March's note. She had come with Rose, and had left him below with March; Mrs. Adding was coming later with Kenby and General Triscoe.

Mrs. March lost no time in telling her the great news; and if she had been in doubt before of the girl's feeling for Burnamy she was now in none. She had the pleasure of seeing her flush with hope, and then the pain which was also a pleasure, of seeing her blanch with dismay.

"I don't know where he is, Mrs. March. I haven't heard a word from him since that night in Carlsbad. I expected—I didn't know but you—"

Mrs. March shook her head. She treated the fact skillfully as something to be regretted simply because it would be such a relief to Burnamy to know how Mr. Stoller now felt. Of course they could reach him somehow; you could always get letters to people in Europe, in the end; and, in fact, it was altogether probable that he was that very instant in Wurzburg; for if the New York-Paris Chronicle had wanted him to write up the Wagner operas, it would certainly want him to write up the manoeuvres. She established his presence in Wurzburg by such an irrefragable chain of reasoning that, at a knock outside, she was just able to kelp back a scream, while she ran to open the door. It was not Burnamy, as in compliance with every nerve it ought to have been, but her husband, who tried to justify his presence by saying that they were all waiting for her and Miss Triscoe, and asked when they were coming.

She frowned him silent, and then shut herself outside with him long enough to whisper, "Say she's got a headache, or anything you please; but don't stop talking here with me, or I shall go wild." She then shut herself in again, with the effect of holding him accountable for the whole affair.

LVI.

General Triscoe could not keep his irritation, at hearing that his daughter was not coming, out of the excuses he made to Mrs. Adding; he said again and again that it must seem like a discourtesy to her. She gayly disclaimed any such notion; she would not hear of putting off their excursion to another day; it had been raining just long enough to give them a reasonable hope of a few hours' drought, and they might not have another dry spell for weeks. She slipped off her jacket after they started, and gave it to Kenby, but she let General Triscoe hold her umbrella over her, while he limped beside her. She seemed to March, as he followed with Rose, to be playing the two men off against each other, with an ease which he wished his wife could be there to see, and to judge aright.

They crossed by the Old Bridge, which is of the earliest years of the seventh century, between rows of saints whose statues surmount the piers. Some are bishops as well as saints; one must have been at Rome in his day, for he wore his long thick beard in the fashion of Michelangelo's Moses. He stretched out toward the passers two fingers of blessing and was unaware of the sparrow which had lighted on them and was giving him the effect of offering it to the public admiration. Squads of soldiers tramping by turned to look and smile, and the dull faces of citizens lighted up at the quaint sight. Some children stopped and remained very quiet, not to scare away the bird; and a cold-faced, spiritual-looking priest paused among them as if doubting whether to rescue the absent-minded bishop from a situation derogatory to his dignity; but he passed on, and then the sparrow suddenly flew off.

Rose Adding had lingered for the incident with March, but they now pushed on, and came up with the others at the end of the bridge, where they found them in question whether they had not better take a carriage and drive to the foot of the hill before they began their climb. March thanked them, but said he was keeping up the terms of his cure, and was getting in all the walking he could. Rose begged his mother not to include him in the driving party; he protested that he was feeling so well, and the walk was doing him good. His mother consented, if he would promise not to get tired, and then she mounted into the two-spanner which had driven instinctively up to their party when their parley began, and General Triscoe took the place beside her, while Kenby, with smiling patience, seated himself in front.

Rose kept on talking with March about Wurzburg and its history, which it seemed he had been reading the night before when he could not sleep. He explained, "We get little histories of the places wherever we go. That's what Mr. Kenby does, you know."

"Oh, yes," said March.

"I don't suppose I shall get a chance to read much here," Rose continued, "with General Triscoe in the room. He doesn't like the light."

"Well, well. He's rather old, you know. And you musn't read too much, Rose. It isn't good for you."

"I know, but if I don't read, I think, and that keeps me awake worse. Of course, I respect General Triscoe for being in the war, and getting wounded," the boy suggested.

"A good many did it," March was tempted to say.

The boy did not notice his insinuation. "I suppose there were some things they did in the army, and then they couldn't get over the habit. But General Grant says in his 'Life' that he never used a profane expletive."

"Does General Triscoe?"

Rose answered reluctantly, "If anything wakes him in the night, or if he can't make these German beds over to suit him—"

"I see." March turned his face to hide the smile which he would not have let the boy detect. He thought best not to let Rose resume his impressions of the general; and in talk of weightier matters they found themselves at that point of the climb where the carriage was waiting for them. From this point they followed an alley through ivied, garden walls, till they reached the first of the balustraded terraces which ascend to the crest of the hill where the church stands. Each terrace is planted with sycamores, and the face of the terrace wall supports a bass-relief commemorating with the drama of its lifesize figures the stations of the cross.

Monks and priests were coming and going, and dropped on the steps leading from terrace to terrace were women and children on their knees in prayer. It was all richly reminiscent of pilgrim scenes in other Catholic lands; but here there was a touch of earnest in the Northern face of the worshipers which the South had never imparted. Even in the beautiful rococo interior of the church at the top of the hill there was a sense of something deeper and truer than mere ecclesiasticism; and March came out of it in a serious muse while the boy at his side did nothing to interrupt. A vague regret filled his heart as he gazed silently out over the prospect of river and city and vineyard, purpling together below the top where he stood, and mixed with this regret was a vague resentment of his wife's absence. She ought to have been there to share his pang and his pleasure; they had so long enjoyed everything together that without her he felt unable to get out of either emotion all there was in it.

The forgotten boy stole silently down the terraces after the rest of the party who had left him behind with March. At the last terrace they stopped and waited; and after a delay that began to be long to Mrs. Adding, she wondered aloud what could have become of them.

Kenby promptly offered to go back and see, and she consented in seeming to refuse: "It isn't worth while. Rose has probably got Mr. March into some deep discussion, and they've forgotten all about us. But if you will go, Mr. Kenby, you might just remind Rose of my existence." She let him lay her jacket on her shoulders before he left her, and then she sat down on one of the steps, which General Triscoe kept striking with the point of her umbrella as he stood before her.

"I really shall have to take it from you if you do that any more," she said, laughing up in his face. "I'm serious."

He stopped. "I wish I could believe you were serious, for a moment."

"You may, if you think it will do you any good. But I don't see why."

The general smiled, but with a kind of tremulous eagerness which might have been pathetic to any one who liked him. "Do you know this is almost the first time I have spoken alone with you?"

"Really, I hadn't noticed," said Mrs. Adding.

General Triscoe laughed in rather a ghastly way. "Well, that's encouraging, at least, to a man who's had his doubts whether it wasn't intended."

"Intended? By whom? What do you mean, General Triscoe? Why in the world shouldn't you have spoken alone with me before?"

He was not, with all his eagerness, ready to say, and while she smiled pleasantly she had the look in her eyes of being brought to bay and being prepared, if it must come to that, to have the worst over, then and there. She was not half his age, but he was aware of her having no respect for his years; compared with her average American past as he understood it, his social place was much higher, but, she was not in the least awed by it; in spite of his war record she was making him behave like a coward. He was in a false position, and if he had any one but himself to blame he had not her. He read her equal knowledge of these facts in the clear eyes that made him flush and turn his own away.

Then he started with a quick "Hello!" and stood staring up at the steps from the terrace above, where Rose Adding was staying himself weakly by a clutch of Kenby on one side and March on the other.

His mother looked round and caught herself up from where she sat and ran toward him. "Oh, Rose!"

"It's nothing, mother," he called to her, and as she dropped on her knees before him he sank limply against her. "It was like what I had in Carlsbad; that's all. Don't worry about me, please!"

"I'm not worrying, Rose," she said with courage of the same texture as his own. "You've been walking too much. You must go back in the carriage with us. Can't you have it come here?" she asked Kenby.

"There's no road, Mrs. Adding. But if Rose would let me carry him—"

"I can walk," the boy protested, trying to lift himself from her neck.

"No, no! you mustn't." She drew away and let him fall into the arms that Kenby put round him. He raised the frail burden lightly to his shoulder, and moved strongly away, followed by the eyes of the spectators who had gathered about the little group, but who dispersed now, and went back to their devotions.

March hurried after Kenby with Mrs. Adding, whom he told he had just missed Rose and was looking about for him, when Kenby came with her message for them. They made sure that he was nowhere about the church, and then started together down the terraces. At the second or third station below they found the boy clinging to the barrier that protected the bass-relief from the zeal of the devotees. He looked white and sick, though he insisted that he was well, and when he turned to come away with them he reeled and would have fallen if Kenby had not caught him. Kenby wanted to carry him, but Rose would not let him, and had made his way down between them.

"Yea, he has such a spirit," she said, "and I've no doubt he's suffering now more from Mr. Kenby's kindness than from his own sickness he had one of these giddy turns in Carlsbad, though, and I shall certainly have a doctor to see him."

"I think I should, Mrs. Adding," said March, not too gravely, for it seemed to him that it was not quite his business to alarm her further, if she was herself taking the affair with that seriousness. He questioned whether she was taking it quite seriously enough, when she turned with a laugh, and called to General Triscoe, who was limping down the steps of the last terrace behind them:

"Oh, poor General Triscoe! I thought you had gone on ahead."

General Triscoe could not enter into the joke of being forgotten, apparently. He assisted with gravity at the disposition of the party for the return, when they all reached the carriage. Rose had the place beside his mother, and Kenby wished March to take his with the general and let him sit with the driver; but he insisted that he would rather walk home, and he did walk till they had driven out of eight. Then he called a passing one-spanner, and drove to his hotel in comfort and silence.

LVII.

Kenby did not come to the Swan before supper; then he reported that the doctor had said Rose was on the verge of a nervous collapse. He had overworked at school, but the immediate trouble was the high, thin air, which the doctor said he must be got out of at once, into a quiet place at the sea-shore somewhere. He had suggested Ostend; or some point on the French coast; Kenby had thought of Schevleningen, and the doctor had said that would do admirably.

"I understood from Mrs. Adding," he concluded, "that you were going. there for your after-cure, Mr. March, and I didn't know but you might be going soon."

At the mention of Schevleningen the Marches had looked at each other with a guilty alarm, which they both tried to give the cast of affectionate sympathy but she dismissed her fear that he might be going to let his compassion prevail with him to his hurt when he said: "Why, we ought to have been there before this, but I've been taking my life in my hands in trying to see a little of Germany, and I'm afraid now that Mrs. March has her mind too firmly fixed on Berlin to let me think of going to Schevleningen till we've been there."

"It's too bad!" said Mrs. March, with real regret. "I wish we were going." But she had not the least notion of gratifying her wish; and they were all silent till Kenby broke out:

"Look here! You know how I feel about Mrs Adding! I've been pretty frank with Mr. March myself, and I've had my suspicions that she's been frank with you, Mrs. March. There isn't any doubt about my wanting to marry her, and up to this time there hasn't been any doubt about her not wanting to marry me. But it isn't a question of her or of me, now. It's a question of Rose. I love the boy," and Kenby's voice shook, and he faltered a moment. "Pshaw! You understand."

"Indeed I do, Mr. Kenby," said Mrs. March. "I perfectly understand you."

"Well, I don't think Mrs. Adding is fit to make the journey with him alone, or to place herself in the best way after she gets to Schevleningen. She's been badly shaken up; she broke down before the doctor; she said she didn't know what to do; I suppose she's frightened—"

Kenby stopped again, and March asked, "When is she going?"

"To-morrow," said Kenby, and he added, "And now the question is, why shouldn't I go with her?"

Mrs. March gave a little start, and looked at her husband, but he said nothing, and Kenby seemed not to have supposed that he would say anything.

"I know it would be very American, and all that, but I happen to be an American, and it wouldn't be out of character for me. I suppose," he appealed to Mrs. March, "that it's something I might offer to do if it were from New York to Florida—and I happened to be going there? And I did happen to be going to Holland."

"Why, of course, Mr. Kenby," she responded, with such solemnity that March gave way in an outrageous laugh.

Kenby laughed, and Mrs. March laughed too, but with an inner note of protest.

"Well," Kenby continued, still addressing her, "what I want you to do is to stand by me when I propose it."

Mrs. March gathered strength to say, "No, Mr. Kenby, it's your own affair, and you must take the responsibility."

"Do you disapprove?"

"It isn't the same as it would be at home. You see that yourself."

"Well," said Kenby, rising, "I have to arrange about their getting away to-morrow. It won't be easy in this hurly-burly that's coming off."

"Give Rose our love; and tell Mrs. Adding that I'll come round and see her to-morrow before she starts."

"Oh! I'm afraid you can't, Mrs. March. They're to start at six in the morning."

"They are! Then we must go and see them tonight. We'll be there almost as soon as you are."

March went up to their rooms with, his wife, and she began on the stairs:

"Well, my dear, I hope you realize that your laughing so gave us completely away. And what was there to keep grinning about, all through?"

"Nothing but the disingenuous, hypocritical passion of love. It's always the most amusing thing in the world; but to see it trying to pass itself off in poor old Kenby as duty and humanity, and disinterested affection for Rose, was more than I could stand. I don't apologize for laughing; I wanted to yell."

His effrontery and his philosophy both helped to save him; and she said from the point where he had side-tracked her mind: "I don't call it disingenuous. He was brutally frank. He's made it impossible to treat the affair with dignity. I want you to leave the whole thing to me, from this out. Now, will you?"

On their way to the Spanischer Hof she arranged in her own mind for Mrs. Adding to get a maid, and for the doctor to send an assistant with her on the journey, but she was in such despair with her scheme that she had not the courage to right herself when Mrs. Adding met her with the appeal:

"Oh, Mrs. March, I'm so glad you approve of Mr. Kenby's plan. It does seem the only thing to do. I can't trust myself alone with Rose, and Mr. Kenby's intending to go to Schevleningen a few days later anyway. Though it's too bad to let him give up the manoeuvres."

"I'm sure he won't mind that," Mrs. March's voice said mechanically, while her thought was busy with the question whether this scandalous duplicity was altogether Kenby's, and whether Mrs. Adding was as guiltless of any share in it as she looked. She looked pitifully distracted; she might not have understood his report; or Kenby might really have mistaken Mrs. March's sympathy for favor.

"No, he only lives to do good," Mrs. Adding returned. "He's with Rose; won't you come in and see them?"

Rose was lying back on the pillows of a sofa, from which they would not let him get up. He was full of the trip to Holland, and had already pushed Kenby, as Kenby owned, beyond the bounds of his very general knowledge of the Dutch language, which Rose had plans for taking up after they were settled in Schevleningen. The boy scoffed at the notion that he was not perfectly well, and he wished to talk with March on the points where he had found Kenby wanting.

"Kenby is an encyclopaedia compared with me, Rose," the editor protested, and he amplified his ignorance for the boy's good to an extent which Rose saw was a joke. He left Holland to talk about other things which his mother thought quite as bad for him. He wished to know if March did not think that the statue of the bishop with the sparrow on its finger was a subject for a poem; and March said gayly that if Rose would write it he would print it in 'Every Other Week'.

The boy flushed with pleasure at his banter. "No, I couldn't do it. But I wish Mr. Burnamy had seen it. He could. Will you tell him about it?" He wanted to know if March had heard from Burnamy lately, and in the midst of his vivid interest he gave a weary sigh.

His mother said that now he had talked enough, and bade him say good-by to the Marches, who were coming so soon to Holland, anyway. Mrs. March put her arms round him to kiss him, and when she let him sink back her eyes were dim.

"You see how frail he is?" said Mrs. Adding. "I shall not let him out of my sight, after this, till he's well again."

She had a kind of authority in sending Kenby away with them which was not lost upon the witnesses. He asked them to come into the reading-room a moment with him, and Mrs. March wondered if he were going to make some excuse to her for himself; but he said: "I don't know how we're to manage about the Triscoes. The general will have a room to himself, but if Mrs. Adding takes Rose in with her, it leaves Miss Triscoe out, and there isn't a room to be had in this house for love or money. Do you think," he appealed directly to Mrs. March, "that it would do to offer her my room at the Swan?"

"Why, yes," she assented, with a reluctance rather for the complicity in which he had already involved her, and for which he was still unpunished, than for what he was now proposing. "Or she could come in with me, and Mr. March could take it."

"Whichever you think," said Kenby so submissively that she relented, to ask:

"And what will you do?"

He laughed. "Well, people have been known to sleep in a chair. I shall manage somehow."

"You might offer to go in with the general," March suggested, and the men apparently thought this was a joke. Mrs. March did not laugh in her feminine worry about ways and means.

"Where is Miss Triscoe?" she asked. "We haven't seen them."

"Didn't Mrs. Adding tell you? They went to supper at a restaurant; the general doesn't like the cooking here. They ought to have been back before this."

He looked up at the clock on the wall, and she said, "I suppose you would like us to wait."

"It would be very kind of you."

"Oh, it's quite essential," she returned with an airy freshness which Kenby did not seem to feel as painfully as he ought.

They all sat down, and the Triscoes came in after a few minutes, and a cloud on the general's face lifted at the proposition Kenby left Mrs. March to make.

"I thought that child ought to be in his mother's charge," he said. With his own comfort provided for, he made no objections to Mrs. March's plan; and Agatha went to take leave of Rose and his mother. "By-the-way," the general turned to March, "I found Stoller at the restaurant where we supped. He offered me a place in his carriage for the manoeuvres. How are you going?"

"I think I shall go by train. I don't fancy the long drive."

"Well, I don't know that it's worse than the long walk after you leave the train," said the general from the offence which any difference of taste was apt to give him. "Are you going by train, too?" he asked Kenby with indifference.

"I'm not going at all," said Kenby. "I'm leaving Wurzburg in the morning."

"Oh, indeed," said the general.

Mrs. March could not make out whether he knew that Kenby was going with Rose and Mrs. Adding, but she felt that there must be a full and open recognition of the fact among them. "Yes," she said, "isn't it fortunate that Mr. Kenby should be going to Holland, too! I should have been so unhappy about them if Mrs. Adding had been obliged to make that long journey with poor little Rose alone."

"Yes, yes; very fortunate, certainly," said the general colorlessly.

Her husband gave her a glance of intelligent appreciation; but Kenby was too simply, too densely content with the situation to know the value of what she had done. She thought he must certainly explain, as he walked back with her to the Swan, whether he had misrepresented her to Mrs. Adding, or Mrs. Adding had misunderstood him. Somewhere there had been an error, or a duplicity which it was now useless to punish; and Kenby was so apparently unconscious of it that she had not the heart to be cross with him. She heard Miss Triscoe behind her with March laughing in the gayety which the escape from her father seemed to inspire in her. She was promising March to go with him in the morning to see the Emperor and Empress of Germany arrive at the station, and he was warning her that if she laughed there, like that, she would subject him to fine and imprisonment. She pretended that she would like to see him led off between two gendarmes, but consented to be a little careful when he asked her how she expected to get back to her hotel without him, if such a thing happened.

LVIII.

After all, Miss Triscoe did not go with March; she preferred to sleep. The imperial party was to arrive at half past seven, but at six the crowd was already dense before the station, and all along the street leading to the Residenz. It was a brilliant day, with the promise of sunshine, through which a chilly wind blew, for the manoeuvres. The colors of all the German states flapped in this breeze from the poles wreathed with evergreen which encircled the square; the workmen putting the last touches on the bronzed allegory hurried madly to be done, and they had, scarcely finished their labors when two troops of dragoons rode into the place and formed before the station, and waited as motionlessly as their horses would allow.

These animals were not so conscious as lions at the approach of princes; they tossed and stamped impatiently in the long interval before the Regent and his daughter-in-law came to welcome their guests. All the human beings, both those who were in charge and those who were under charge, were in a quiver of anxiety to play their parts well, as if there were some heavy penalty for failure in the least point. The policemen keeping the people, in line behind the ropes which restrained them trembled with eagerness; the faces of some of the troopers twitched. An involuntary sigh went up from the crowd as the Regent's carriage appeared, heralded by outriders, and followed by other plain carriages of Bavarian blue with liveries of blue and silver. Then the whistle of the Kaiser's train sounded; a trumpeter advanced and began to blow his trumpet as they do in the theatre; and exactly at the appointed moment the Emperor and Empress came out of the station through the brilliant human alley leading from it, mounted their carriages, with the stage trumpeter always blowing, and whirled swiftly round half the square and flashed into the corner toward the Residenz out of sight. The same hollow groans of Ho-o-o-ch greeted and followed them from the spectators as had welcomed the Regent when he first arrived among his fellow-townsmen, with the same effect of being the conventional cries of a stage mob behind the scenes.

The Emperor was like most of his innumerable pictures, with a swarthy face from which his blue eyes glanced pleasantly; he looked good-humored if not good-natured; the Empress smiled amiably beneath her deeply fringed white parasol, and they both bowed right and left in acknowledgment of those hollow groans; but again it seemed, to March that sovereignty, gave the popular curiosity, not to call it devotion, a scantier return than it merited. He had perhaps been insensibly working toward some such perception as now came to him that the great difference between Europe and America was that in Europe life is histrionic and dramatized, and that in America, except when it is trying to be European, it is direct and sincere. He wondered whether the innate conviction of equality, the deep, underlying sense of a common humanity transcending all social and civic pretences, was what gave their theatrical effect to the shows of deference from low to high, and of condescension from high to low. If in such encounters of sovereigns and subjects, the prince did not play his part so well as the people, it might be that he had a harder part to play, and that to support his dignity at all, to keep from being found out the sham that he essentially was, he had to hurry across the stage amidst the distracting thunders of the orchestra. If the star staid to be scrutinized by the soldiers, citizens, and so forth, even the poor supernumeraries and scene-shifters might see that he was a tallow candle like themselves.

In the censorious mood induced by the reflection that he had waited an hour and a half for half a minute's glimpse of the imperial party, March now decided not to go to the manoeuvres, where he might be subjected to still greater humiliation and disappointment. He had certainly come to Wurzburg for the manoeuvres, but Wurzburg had been richly repaying in itself; and why should he stifle half an hour in an overcrowded train, and struggle for three miles on foot against that harsh wind, to see a multitude of men give proofs of their fitness to do manifold murder? He was, in fact, not the least curious for the sight, and the only thing that really troubled him was the question of how he should justify his recreance to his wife. This did alloy the pleasure with which he began, after an excellent breakfast at a neighboring cafe, to stroll about the streets, though he had them almost to himself, so many citizens had followed the soldiers to the manoeuvres.

It was not till the soldiers began returning from the manoeuvres, dusty-footed, and in white canvas overalls drawn over their trousers to save them, that he went back to Mrs. March and Miss Triscoe at the Swan. He had given them time enough to imagine him at the review, and to wonder whether he had seen General Triscoe and the Stollers there, and they met him with such confident inquiries that he would not undeceive them at once. He let them divine from his inventive answers that he had not gone to the manoeuvres, which put them in the best humor with themselves, and the girl said it was so cold and rough that she wished her father had not gone, either. The general appeared just before dinner and frankly avowed the same wish. He was rasping and wheezing from the dust which filled his lungs; he looked blown and red, and he was too angry with the company he had been in to have any comments on the manoeuvres. He referred to the military chiefly in relation to the Miss Stollers' ineffectual flirtations, which he declared had been outrageous. Their father had apparently no control over them whatever, or else was too ignorant to know that they were misbehaving. They were without respect or reverence for any one; they had talked to General Triscoe as if he were a boy of their own age, or a dotard whom nobody need mind;

they had not only kept up their foolish babble before him, they had laughed and giggled, they had broken into snatches of American song, they had all but whistled and danced. They made loud comments in Illinois English—on the cuteness of the officers whom they admired, and they had at one time actually got out their handkerchiefs. He supposed they meant to wave them at the officers, but at the look he gave them they merely put their hats together and snickered in derision of him. They were American girls of the worst type; they conformed to no standard of behavior; their conduct was personal. They ought to be taken home.

Mrs. March said she saw what he meant, and she agreed with him that they were altogether unformed, and were the effect of their own ignorant caprices. Probably, however, it was too late to amend them by taking them away.

"It would hide them, at any rate," he answered. "They would sink back into the great mass of our vulgarity, and not be noticed. We behave like a parcel of peasants with our women. We think that if no harm is meant or thought, we may risk any sort of appearance, and we do things that are scandalously improper simply because they are innocent. That may be all very well at home, but people who prefer that sort of thing had better stay there, where our peasant manners won't make them conspicuous."

As their train ran northward out of Wurzburg that afternoon, Mrs. March recurred to the general's closing words. "That was a slap at Mrs. Adding for letting Kenby go off with her."

She took up the history of the past twenty-four hours, from the time March had left her with Miss Triscoe when he went with her father and the Addings and Kenby to see that church. She had had no chance to bring up these arrears until now, and she atoned to herself for the delay by making the history very full, and going back and adding touches at any point where she thought she had scanted it. After all, it consisted mainly of fragmentary intimations from Miss Triscoe and of half-uttered questions which her own art now built into a coherent statement.

March could not find that the general had much resented Burnamy's clandestine visit to Carlsbad when his daughter told him of it, or that he had done more than make her promise that she would not keep up the acquaintance upon any terms unknown to him.

"Probably," Mrs. March said, "as long as he had any hopes of Mrs. Adding, he was a little too self-conscious to be very up and down about Burnamy."

"Then you think he was really serious about her?"

"Now my dear! He was so serious that I suppose he was never so completely taken aback in his life as when he met Kenby in Wurzburg and saw how she received him. Of course, that put an end to the fight."

"The fight?"

"Yes—that Mrs. Adding and Agatha were keeping up to prevent his offering himself."

"Oh! And how do you know that they were keeping up the fight together?"

"How do I? Didn't you see yourself what friends they were? Did you tell him what Stoller had, said about Burnamy?"

"I had no chance. I don't know that I should have done it, anyway. It wasn't my affair."

"Well, then, I think you might. It would have been everything for that poor child; it would have completely justified her in her own eyes."

"Perhaps your telling her will serve the same purpose."

"Yes, I did tell her, and I am glad of it. She had a right to know it."

"Did she think Stoller's willingness to overlook Burnamy's performance had anything to do with its moral quality?"

Mrs. March was daunted for the moment, but she said, "I told her you thought that if a person owned to a fault they disowned it, and put it away from them just as if it had never been committed; and that if a person had taken their punishment for a wrong they had done, they had expiated it so far as anybody else was concerned. And hasn't poor Burnamy done both?"

As a moralist March was flattered to be hoist with his own petard, but as a husband he was not going to come down at once. "I thought probably you had told her that. You had it pat from having just been over it with me. When has she heard from him?"

"Why, that's the strangest thing about it. She hasn't heard at all. She doesn't know where he is. She thought we must know. She was terribly broken up."

"How did she show it?"

"She didn't show it. Either you want to tease, or you've forgotten how such things are with young people—or at least girls."

"Yes, it's all a long time ago with me, and I never was a girl. Besides, the frank and direct behavior of Kenby and Mrs. Adding has been very obliterating to my early impressions of love-making."

"It certainly hasn't been ideal," said Mrs. March with a sigh.

"Why hasn't it been ideal?" he asked. "Kenby is tremendously in love with her; and I believe she's had a fancy for him from the beginning. If it hadn't been for Rose she would have accepted him at once; and now he's essential to them both in their helplessness. As for Papa Triscoe and his Europeanized scruples, if they have any reality at all they're the residuum of his personal resentment, and Kenby and Mrs. Adding have nothing to do with their unreality. His being in love with her is no reason why he shouldn't be helpful to her when she needs him, and every reason why he should. I call it a poem, such as very few people have the luck to live out together."

Mrs. March listened with mounting fervor, and when he stopped, she cried out, "Well, my dear, I do believe you are right! It is ideal, as you say; it's a perfect poem. And I shall always say—"

She stopped at the mocking light which she caught in his look, and perceived that he had been amusing himself with her perennial enthusiasm for all sorts of love-affairs. But she averred that she did not care; what he had said was true, and she should always hold him to it.

They were again in the wedding-journey sentiment in which they had left Carlsbad, when they found themselves alone together after their escape from the pressure of others' interests. The tide of travel was towards Frankfort, where the grand parade was to take place some days later. They were going to Weimar, which was so few hours out of their way that they simply must not miss it; and all the way to the old literary capital they were alone in their compartment, with not even a stranger, much less a friend to molest them. The flying landscape without was of their own early autumnal mood, and when the vineyards of Wurzburg ceased to purple it, the heavy after-math of hay and clover, which men, women, and children were loading on heavy wains, and driving from the meadows everywhere, offered a pastoral and pleasing change. It was always the German landscape; sometimes flat and fertile, sometimes hilly and poor; often clothed with dense woods, but always charming, with castled tops in ruin or repair, and with levels where Gothic villages drowsed within their walls, and dreamed of the mediaeval past, silent, without apparent life, except for some little goose-girl driving her flock before her as she sallied out into the nineteenth century in search of fresh pasturage.

As their train mounted among the Thuringian uplands they were aware of a finer, cooler air through their open window. The torrents foamed white out of the black forests of fir and pine, and brawled along the valleys, where the hamlets roused themselves in momentary curiosity as the train roared into them from the many tunnels. The afternoon sunshine had the glister of mountain sunshine everywhere, and the travellers had a pleasant bewilderment in which their memories of Switzerland and the White

Mountains mixed with long-dormant emotions from Adirondack sojourns. They chose this place and that in the lovely region where they lamented that they had not come at once for the after-cure, and they appointed enough returns to it in future years to consume all the summers they had left to live.

LIX.

It was falling night when they reached Weimar, where they found at the station a provision of omnibuses far beyond the hotel accommodations. They drove first to the Crown-Prince, which was in a promising state of reparation, but which for the present could only welcome them to an apartment where a canvas curtain cut them off from a freshly plastered wall. The landlord deplored the fact, and sent hospitably out to try and place them at the Elephant. But the Elephant was full, and the Russian Court was full too. Then the landlord of the Crown-Prince bethought himself of a new hotel, of the second class, indeed, but very nice, where they might get rooms, and after the delay of an hour, they got a carriage and drove away from the Crown-Prince, where the landlord continued to the last as benevolent as if they had been a profit instead of a loss to him.

The streets of the town at nine o'clock were empty and quiet, and they instantly felt the academic quality of the place. Through the pale night they could see that the architecture was of the classic sentiment which they were destined to feel more and more; at one point they caught a fleeting glimpse of two figures with clasped hands and half embraced, which they knew for the statues of Goethe and Schiller; and when they mounted to their rooms at the Grand-Duke of Saxe-Weimar, they passed under a fresco representing Goethe and four other world-famous poets, Shakspere, Milton, Tasso, and Schiller. The poets all looked like Germans, as was just, and Goethe was naturally chief among them; he marshalled the immortals on their way, and Schiller brought up the rear and kept them from going astray in an Elysium where they did not speak the language. For the rest, the hotel was brand-new, of a quite American freshness, and was pervaded by a sweet smell as of straw matting, and provided with steam-radiators. In the sense of its homelikeness the Marches boasted that they were never going away from it.

In the morning they discovered that their windows looked out on the grand-ducal museum, with a gardened space before and below its classicistic bulk, where, in a whim of the weather, the gay flowers were full of sun. In a pleasant illusion of taking it unawares, March strolled up through the town; but Weimar was as much awake at that hour as at any of the twenty-four, and the tranquillity of its streets, where he encountered a few passers several blocks apart, was their habitual mood. He came promptly upon two objects which he would willingly have shunned: a 'denkmal' of the Franco-German war, not so furiously bad as most German monuments, but antipathetic and uninteresting, as all patriotic monuments are; and a woman-and-dog team. In the shock from this he was sensible that he had not seen any woman-and-dog teams for some time, and he wondered by what civic or ethnic influences their distribution was so controlled that they should have abounded in

Hamburg, Leipsic, and Carlsbad, and wholly ceased in Nuremberg, Ansbach, and Wurzburg, to reappear again in Weimar, though they seemed as characteristic of all Germany as the ugly denkmals to her victories over France.

The Goethe and Schiller monument which he had glimpsed the night before was characteristic too, but less offensively so. German statues at the best are conscious; and the poet-pair, as the inscription calls them, have the air of showily confronting posterity with their clasped hands, and of being only partially rapt from the spectators. But they were more unconscious than any other German statues that March had seen, and he quelled a desire to ask Goethe, as he stood with his hand on Schiller's shoulder, and looked serenely into space far above one of the typical equipages of his country, what he thought of that sort of thing. But upon reflection he did not know why Goethe should be held personally responsible for the existence of the woman-and-dog team. He felt that he might more reasonably attribute to his taste the prevalence of classic profiles which he began to note in the Weimar populace. This could be a sympathetic effect of that passion for the antique which the poet brought back with him from his sojourn in Italy; though many of the people, especially the children, were bow-legged. Perhaps the antique had: begun in their faces, and had not yet got down to their legs; in any case they were charming children, and as a test of their culture, he had a mind to ask a little girl if she could tell him where the statue of Herder was, which he thought he might as well take in on his ramble, and so be done with as many statues as he could. She answered with a pretty regret in her tender voice, "That I truly cannot," and he was more satisfied than if she could, for he thought it better to be a child and honest, than to know where any German statue was.

He easily found it for himself in the place which is called the Herder Platz after it. He went into the Peter and Paul Church there; where Herder used to preach sermons, sometimes not at all liked by the nobility and gentry for their revolutionary tendency; the sovereign was shielded from the worst effects of his doctrine by worshipping apart from other sinners in a glazed gallery. Herder is buried in the church, and when you ask where, the sacristan lifts a wooden trap-door in the pavement, and you think you are going down into the crypt, but you are only to see Herder's monumental stone, which is kept covered so to save it from passing feet. Here also is the greatest picture of that great soul Luke Kranach, who had sincerity enough in his paining to atone for all the swelling German sculptures in the world. It is a crucifixion, and the cross is of a white birch log, such as might have been cut out of the Weimar woods, shaved smooth on the sides, with the bark showing at the edges. Kranach has put himself among the spectators, and a stream of blood from the side of the Savior falls in baptism upon the painter's head. He is in the company of John the Baptist and Martin Luther; Luther stands with his Bible open, and his finger on the line, "The blood of Jesus cleanseth us."

Partly because he felt guilty at doing all these things without his wife, and partly because he was now very hungry, March turned from them and got back to his hotel, where she was looking out for him from their open window. She had the air of being long domesticated there, as she laughed down at seeing him come; and the continued brilliancy of the weather added to the illusion of home.

It was like a day of late spring in Italy or America; the sun in that gardened hollow before the museum was already hot enough to make him glad of the shelter of the hotel. The summer seemed to have come back to oblige them, and when they learned that they were to see Weimar in a festive mood because this was Sedan Day, their curiosity, if not their sympathy, accepted the chance gratefully. But they were almost moved to wish that the war had gone otherwise when they learned that all the public carriages were engaged, and they must have one from a stable if they wished to drive after breakfast. Still it was offered them for such a modest number of marks, and their driver proved so friendly and conversable, that they assented to the course of history, and were more and more reconciled as they bowled along through the grand-ducal park beside the waters of the classic Ilm.

The waters of the classic Ilm are sluggish and slimy in places, and in places clear and brooklike, but always a dull dark green in color. They flow in the shadow of pensive trees, and by the brinks of sunny meadows, where the after-math wanders in heavy windrows, and the children sport joyously over the smooth-mown surfaces in all the freedom that there is in Germany. At last, after immemorial appropriation the owners of the earth are everywhere expropriated, and the people come into the pleasure if not the profit of it. At last, the prince, the knight, the noble finds, as in his turn the plutocrat will find, that his property is not for him, but for all; and that the nation is to enjoy what he takes from it and vainly thinks to keep from it. Parks, pleasaunces, gardens, set apart for kings, are the play-grounds of the landless poor in the Old World, and perhaps yield the sweetest joy of privilege to some state-sick ruler, some world-weary princess, some lonely child born to the solitude of sovereignty, as they each look down from their palace windows upon the leisure of overwork taking its little holiday amidst beauty vainly created for the perpetual festival of their empty lives.

March smiled to think that in this very Weimar, where sovereignty had graced and ennobled itself as nowhere else in the world by the companionship of letters and the arts, they still were not hurrying first to see the palace of a prince, but were involuntarily making it second to the cottage of a poet. But in fact it is Goethe who is forever the prince in Weimar. His greatness blots out its history, his name fills the city; the thought of him is its chiefest imitation and largest hospitality. The travellers remembered, above all other facts of the grand-ducal park, that it was there he first met Christiane Vulpius, beautiful and young, when he too was beautiful and young, and took her home to be his love, to the just and lasting displeasure of Fran von Stein, who was even less reconciled when, after eighteen years of due reflection, the love of Goethe and Christiane became their marriage. They, wondered just where it was he saw the young girl coming to meet him as the Grand-Duke's minister with an office-seeking petition from her brother, Goethe's brother author, long famed and long forgotten for his romantic tale of "Rinaldo Rinaldini."

They had indeed no great mind, in their American respectability, for that rather matter-of-fact and deliberate liaison, and little as their sympathy was for the passionless intellectual intrigue with the Frau von Stein, it cast no halo of sentiment about the Goethe cottage to suppose that there his love-life with Christiane began. Mrs. March even resented the fact, and when she learned later that it was not the fact at all, she removed it from her associations with the pretty place almost indignantly.

In spite of our facile and multiple divorces we Americans are worshipers of marriage, and if a great poet, the minister of a prince, is going to marry a poor girl, we think he had better not wait till their son is almost of age. Mrs. March would not accept as extenuating circumstances the Grand-Duke's godfatherhood, or Goethe's open constancy to Christiane, or the tardy consecration of their union after the French sack of, Weimar, when the girl's devotion had saved him from the rudeness of the marauding soldiers. For her New England soul there were no degrees in such guilt; and, perhaps there are really not so many as people have tried to think, in their deference to Goethe's greatness. But certainly the affair was not so simple for a grand-ducal minister of world-wide renown, and he might well have felt its difficulties, for he could not have been proof against the censorious public opinion of Weimar, or the yet more censorious private opinion of Fran von Stein.

On that lovely Italo-American morning no ghost of these old dead embarrassments lingered within or without the Goethe garden-house. The trees which the poet himself planted flung a sun-shot shadow upon it, and about its feet basked a garden of simple flowers, from which the sweet lame girl who limped through the rooms and showed them, gathered a parting nosegay for her visitors. The few small livingrooms were above the ground-floor, with kitchen and offices below in the Italian fashion; in one of the little chambers was the camp-bed which Goethe carried with him on his journeys through Italy; and in the larger room at the front stood the desk where he wrote, with the chair before it from which he might just have risen.

All was much more livingly conscious of the great man gone than the proud little palace in the town, which so abounds with relics and memorials of him. His library, his study, his study table, with everything on it just as he left it when

"Cadde la stanca mana"

are there, and there is the death-chair facing the window, from which he gasped for "more light" at last. The handsome, well-arranged rooms are full of souvenirs of his travel, and of that passion for Italy which he did so much to impart to all German hearts, and whose modern waning leaves its records here of an interest pathetically, almost amusingly, faded. They intimate the classic temper to which his mind tended more and more, and amidst the multitude of sculptures, pictures, prints, drawings, gems, medals, autographs, there is the sense of the many-mindedness, the universal taste, for which he found room in little Weimar, but not in his contemporaneous Germany. But it is all less keenly personal, less intimate than the simple garden-house, or else, with the great troop of people going through it, and the custodians lecturing in various voices and languages to the attendant groups, the Marches had it less to themselves, and so imagined him less in it.

LX.

All palaces have a character of tiresome unlivableness which is common to them everywhere, and very probably if one could meet their proprietors in them one would as little remember them apart afterwards as the palaces themselves. It will not do to lift either houses or men far out of the average; they become spectacles, ceremonies; they cease to have charm, to have character, which belong to the levels of life, where alone there are ease and comfort, and human nature may be itself, with all the little delightful differences repressed in those who represent and typify.

As they followed the custodian through the grand-ducal Residenz at Weimar, March felt everywhere the strong wish of the prince who was Goethe's friend to ally himself with literature, and to be human at least in the humanities. He came honestly by his passion for poets; his mother had known it in her time, and Weimar was the home of Wieland and of Herder before the young Grand-Duke came back from his travels bringing Goethe with him, and afterwards attracting Schiller. The story of that great epoch is all there in the Residenz, told as articulately as a palace can.

There are certain Poets' Rooms, frescoed with illustrations of Goethe, Schiller, and Wieland; there is the room where Goethe and the Grand-Duke used to play chess together; there is the conservatory opening from it where they liked to sit and chat; everywhere in the pictures and sculptures, the engraving and intaglios, are the witnesses of the tastes they shared, the love they both had for Italy, and for beautiful Italian things. The prince was not so great a prince but that he could very nearly be a man; the court was perhaps the most human court that ever was; the Grand-Duke and the grand poet were first boon companions, and then monarch and minister working together for the good of the country; they were always friends, and yet, as the American saw in the light of the New World, which he carried with him, how far from friends! At best it was make-believe, the make-believe of superiority and inferiority, the make-believe of master and man, which could only be the more painful and ghastly for the endeavor of two generous spirits to reach and rescue each other through the asphyxiating unreality; but they kept up the show of equality faithfully to the end. Goethe was born citizen of a free republic, and his youth was nurtured in the traditions of liberty; he was one of the greatest souls of any time, and he must have known the impossibility of the thing they pretended; but he died and made no sign, and the poet's friendship with the prince has passed smoothly into history as one of the things that might really be. They worked and played together; they dined and danced, they picnicked and poetized, each on his own side of the impassable gulf; with an air of its not being there which probably did not deceive their contemporaries so much as posterity.

A part of the palace was of course undergoing repair; and in the gallery beyond the conservatory a company of workmen were sitting at a table where they had spread their luncheon. They were somewhat subdued by the consciousness of their august environment; but the sight of them was charming; they gave a kindly interest to the place which it had wanted before; and which the Marches felt again in another palace where the custodian showed them the little tin dishes and saucepans which the German Empress Augusta and her sisters played with when they were children. The sight of these was more affecting even than the withered wreaths which they had left on the death-bed of their mother, and which are still mouldering there.

This was in the Belvedere, the country house on the height overlooking Weimar, where the grand-ducal family spend the month of May, and where the stranger finds himself amid overwhelming associations of Goethe, although the place is so full of relics and memorials of the owners. It seemed in fact to be a storehouse for the wedding-presents of the whole connection, which were on show in every room; Mrs. March hardly knew whether they heightened the domestic effect or took from it; but they enabled her to verify with the custodian's help certain royal intermarriages which she had been in doubt about before.

Her zeal for these made such favor with him that he did not spare them a portrait of all those which March hoped to escape; he passed them over, scarcely able to stand, to the gardener, who was to show them the open-air theatre where Goethe used to take part in the plays.

The Natur-Theater was of a classic ideal, realized in the trained vines and clipped trees which formed the coulisses. There was a grassy space for the chorus and the commoner audience, and then a few semicircular gradines cut in the turf, one alcove another, where the more honored spectators sat. Behind the seats were plinths bearing the busts of Goethe, Schiller, Wieland, and Herder. It was all very pretty, and if ever the weather in Weimar was dry enough to permit a performance, it must have been charming to see a play in that open day to which the drama is native, though in the late hours it now keeps in the thick air of modern theatres it has long forgotten the fact. It would be difficult to be Greek under a German sky, even when it was not actually raining, but March held that with Goethe's help it might have been done at Weimar, and his wife and he proved themselves such enthusiasts for the Natur-Theater that the walnut-faced old gardener who showed it put together a sheaf of the flowers that grew nearest it and gave them to Mrs. March for a souvenir.

They went for a cup of tea to the cafe which looks, as from another eyebrow of the hill, out over lovely little Weimar in the plain below. In a moment of sunshine the prospect was very smiling; but their spirits sank over their tea when it came; they were at least sorry they had not asked for coffee. Most of the people about them were taking beer, including the pretty girls of a young ladies' school, who were there with their books and needle-work, in the care of one of the teachers, apparently for the afternoon.

Mrs. March perceived that they were not so much engaged with their books or their needle-work but they had eyes for other things, and she followed the glances of the girls till they rested upon the people at a table somewhat obliquely to the left. These were apparently a mother and daughter, and they were listening to a young man who sat with his back to Mrs. March, and leaned low over the table talking to them. They were both smiling radiantly, and as the girl smiled she kept turning herself from the waist up, and slanting her face from this side to that, as if to make sure that every one saw her smiling.

Mrs. March felt her husband's gaze following her own, and she had just time to press her finger firmly on his arm and reduce his cry of astonishment to the hoarse whisper in which he gasped, "Good gracious! It's the pivotal girl!"

At the same moment the girl rose with her mother, and with the young man, who had risen too, came directly toward the Marches on their way out of the place without noticing them, though Burnamy passed so near that Mrs. March could almost have touched him.

She had just strength to say, "Well, my dear! That was the cut direct."

She said this in order to have her husband reassure her. "Nonsense! He never saw us. Why didn't you speak to him?"

"Speak to him? I never shall speak to him again. No! This is the last of Mr. Burnamy for me. I shouldn't have minded his not recognizing us, for, as you say, I don't believe he saw us; but if he could go back to such a girl as that, and flirt with her, after Miss Triscoe, that's all I wish to know of him. Don't you try to look him up, Basil! I'm glad-yes, I'm glad he doesn't know how Stoller has come to feel about him; he deserves to suffer, and I hope he'll keep on suffering: You were quite right, my dear—and it shows how true your instinct is in such things (I don't call it more than instinct)—not to tell him what Stoller said, and I don't want you ever should."

She had risen in her excitement, and was making off in such haste that she would hardly give him time to pay for their tea, as she pulled him impatiently to their carriage.

At last he got a chance to say, "I don't think I can quite promise that; my mind's been veering round in the other direction. I think I shall tell him."

"What! After you've seen him flirting with that girl? Very well, then, you won't, my dear; that's all! He's behaving very basely to Agatha."

"What's his flirtation with all the girls in the universe to do with my duty to him? He has a right to know what Stoller thinks. And as to his behaving badly toward Miss Triscoe, how has he done it? So far as you know, there is nothing whatever between them. She either refused him outright, that last night in Carlsbad, or else she made impossible conditions with him. Burnamy is simply consoling himself, and I don't blame him."

"Consoling himself with a pivotal girl!" cried Mrs. March.

"Yes, with a pivotal girl. Her pivotality may be a nervous idiosyncrasy, or it may be the effect of tight lacing; perhaps she has to keep turning and twisting that way to get breath. But attribute the worst motive: say it is to make people look at her! Well, Burnamy has a right to look with the rest; and I am not going to renounce him because he takes refuge with one pretty girl from another. It's what men have been doing from the beginning of time."

"Oh, I dare say!"

"Men," he went on, "are very delicately constituted; very peculiarly. They have been known to seek the society of girls in general, of any girl, because some girl has made them happy; and when some girl has made them unhappy, they are still more susceptible. Burnamy may be merely amusing himself, or he may be consoling himself; but in either case I think the pivotal girl has as much right to him as Miss Triscoe. She had him first; and I'm all for her."

LXI.

Burnamy came away from seeing the pivotal girl and her mother off on the train which they were taking that evening for Frankfort and Hombourg, and strolled back through the Weimar streets little at ease with himself. While he was with the girl and near her he had felt the attraction by which youth impersonally draws youth, the charm which mere maid has for mere man; but once beyond the range of this he felt sick at heart and ashamed. He was aware of having used her folly as an anodyne for the pain which was always gnawing at him, and he had managed to forget it in her folly, but now it came back, and the sense that he had been reckless of her rights came with it. He had done his best to make her think him in love with her, by everything but words; he wondered how he could be such an ass, such a wicked ass, as to try making her promise to write to him from Frankfort; he wished never to see her again, and he wished still less to hear from her. It was some comfort to reflect that she had not promised, but it was not comfort enough to restore him to such fragmentary self-respect as he had been enjoying since he parted with Agatha Triscoe in Carlsbad; he could not even get back to the resentment with which he had been staying himself somewhat before the pivotal girl unexpectedly appeared with her mother in Weimar.

It was Sedan Day, but there was apparently no official observance of the holiday, perhaps because the Grand-Duke was away at the manoeuvres, with all the other German princes. Burnamy had hoped for some voluntary excitement among the people, at least enough to warrant him in making a paper about Sedan Day in Weimar, which he could sell somewhere; but the night was falling, and there was still no sign of popular rejoicing over the French humiliation twenty-eight years before, except in the multitude of Japanese lanterns which the children were everywhere carrying at the ends of sticks. Babies had them in their carriages, and the effect of the floating lights in the winding, up-and-down-hill streets was charming even to Burnamy's lack-lustre eyes. He went by his hotel and on to a cafe with a garden, where there was a patriotic, concert promised; he supped there, and then sat dreamily behind his beer, while the music banged and brayed round him unheeded.

Presently he heard a voice of friendly banter saying in English, "May I sit at your table?" and he saw an ironical face looking down on him. "There doesn't seem any other place."

"Why, Mr. March!" Burnamy sprang up and wrung the hand held out to him, but he choked with his words of recognition; it was so good to see this faithful friend again, though he saw him now as he had seen him last, just when he had so little reason to be proud of himself.

March settled his person in the chair facing Burnamy, and then glanced round at the joyful jam of people eating and drinking, under a firmament of lanterns. "This is pretty," he said, "mighty pretty. I shall make Mrs. March sorry for not coming, when I go back."

"Is Mrs. March—she is—with you—in Weimar?" Burnamy asked stupidly.

March forbore to take advantage of him. "Oh, yes. We saw you out at Belvedere this afternoon. Mrs. March thought for a moment that you meant not to see us. A woman likes to exercise her imagination in those little flights."

"I never dreamed of your being there—I never saw—" Burnamy began.

"Of course not. Neither did Mrs. Etkins, nor Miss Etkins; she was looking very pretty. Have you been here some time?"

"Not long. A week or so. I've been at the parade at Wurzburg."

"At Wurzburg! Ah, how little the world is, or how large Wurzburg is! We were there nearly a week, and we pervaded the place. But there was a great crowd for you to hide in from us. What had I better take?" A waiter had come up, and was standing at March's elbow. "I suppose I mustn't sit here without ordering something?"

"White wine and selters," said Burnamy vaguely.

"The very thing! Why didn't I think of it? It's a divine drink: it satisfies without filling. I had it a night or two before we left home, in the Madison Square Roof Garden. Have you seen 'Every Other Week' lately?"

"No," said Burnamy, with more spirit than he had yet shown.

"We've just got our mail from Nuremberg. The last number has a poem in it that I rather like." March laughed to see the young fellow's face light up with joyful consciousness. "Come round to my hotel, after you're tired here, and I'll let you see it. There's no hurry. Did you notice the little children with their lanterns, as you came along? It's the gentlest effect that a warlike memory ever came to. The French themselves couldn't have minded those innocents carrying those soft lights on the day of their disaster. You ought to get something out of that, and I've got a subject in trust for you from Rose Adding. He and his mother were at Wurzburg; I'm sorry to say the poor little chap didn't seem very well. They've gone to Holland for the sea air." March had been talking for quantity in compassion of the embarrassment in which Burnamy seemed bound; but he questioned how far he ought to bring comfort to the young fellow merely because he liked him. So far as he could make out, Burnamy had been doing rather less than nothing to retrieve himself since they had met; and it was by an impulse that he could not have logically defended to Mrs. March that he resumed. "We found another friend of yours in Wurzburg: Mr. Stoller."

"Mr. Stoller?" Burnamy faintly echoed.

"Yes; he was there to give his daughters a holiday during the manoeuvres; and they made the most of it. He wanted us to go to the parade with his family but we declined. The twins were pretty nearly the death of General Triscoe."

Again Burnamy echoed him. "General Triscoe?"

"Ah, yes: I didn't tell you. General Triscoe and his daughter had come on with Mrs. Adding and Rose. Kenby—you remember Kenby, On the Norumbia?—Kenby happened to be there, too; we were quite a family party; and Stoller got the general to drive out to the manoeuvres with him and his girls."

Now that he was launched, March rather enjoyed letting himself go. He did not know what he should say to Mrs. March when he came to confess having told Burnamy everything before she got a chance at him; he pushed on recklessly, upon the principle, which probably will not hold in morals, that one may as well be hung for a sheep as a lamb. "I have a message for you from Mr. Stoller."

"For me?" Burnamy gasped.

"I've been wondering how I should put it, for I hadn't expected to see you. But it's simply this: he wants you to know—and he seemed to want me to know—that he doesn't hold you accountable in the way he did. He's thought it all over, and he's decided that he had no right to expect you to save him from his own ignorance where he was making a show of knowledge. As he said, he doesn't choose to plead the baby act. He says that you're all right, and your place on the paper is open to you."

Burnamy had not been very prompt before, but now he seemed braced for instant response. "I think he's wrong," he said, so harshly that the people at the next table looked round. "His feeling as he does has nothing to do with the fact, and it doesn't let me out."

March would have liked to take him in his arms; he merely said, "I think you're quite right, as to that. But there's such a thing as forgiveness, you know. It doesn't change the nature of what you've done; but as far as the sufferer from it is concerned, it annuls it."

"Yes, I understand that. But I can't accept his forgiveness if I hate him."

"But perhaps you won't always hate him. Some day you may have a chance to do him a good turn. It's rather banale; but there doesn't seem any other way. Well, I have given you his message. Are you going with me to get that poem?"

When March had given Burnamy the paper at his hotel, and Burnamy had put it in his pocket, the young man said he thought he would take some coffee, and he asked March to join him in the dining-room where they had stood talking.

"No, thank you," said the elder, "I don't propose sitting up all night, and you'll excuse me if I go to bed now. It's a little informal to leave a guest—"

"You're not leaving a guest! I'm at home here. I'm staying in this hotel too."

March said, "Oh!" and then he added abruptly, "Good-night," and went up stairs under the fresco of the five poets.

"Whom were you talking with below?" asked Mrs. March through the door opening into his room from hers.

"Burnamy," he answered from within. "He's staying in this house. He let me know just as I was going to turn him out for the night. It's one of those little uncandors of his that throw suspicion on his honesty in great things."

"Oh! Then you've been telling him," she said, with a mental bound high above and far beyond the point.

"Everything."

"About Stoller, too?"

"About Stoller and his daughters, and Mrs. Adding and Rose and Kenby and General Triscoe—and Agatha."

"Very well. That's what I call shabby. Don't ever talk to me again about the inconsistencies of women. But now there's something perfectly fearful."

"What is it?"

"A letter from Miss Triscoe came after you were gone, asking us to find rooms in some hotel for her and her father to-morrow. He isn't well, and they're coming. And I've telegraphed them to come here. Now what do you say?"

LXII.

They could see no way out of the trouble, and Mrs. March could not resign herself to it till her husband suggested that she should consider it providential. This touched the lingering superstition in which she had been ancestrally taught to regard herself as a means, when in a very tight place, and to leave the responsibility with the moral government of the universe. As she now perceived, it had been the same as ordered that they should see Burnamy under such conditions in the afternoon that they could not speak to him, and hear where he was staying; and in an inferior degree it had been the same as ordered that March should see him in the evening and tell him everything, so that she should know just how to act when she saw him in the morning. If he could plausibly account for the renewal of his flirtation with Miss Elkins, or if he seemed generally worthy apart from that, she could forgive him.

It was so pleasant when he came in at breakfast with his well-remembered smile, that she did not require from him any explicit defence. While they talked she was righting herself in an undercurrent of drama with Miss Triscoe, and explaining to her that they could not possibly wait over for her and her father in Weimar, but must be off that day for Berlin, as they had made all their plans. It was not easy, even in drama where one has everything one's own way, to prove that she could not without impiety so far interfere with the course of Providence as to prevent Miss Triscoe's coming with her father to the same hotel where Burnamy was staying. She contrived, indeed, to persuade her that she had not known he was staying there when she telegraphed them where to come, and that in the absence of any open confidence from Miss Triscoe she was not obliged to suppose that his presence would be embarrassing.

March proposed leaving her with Burnamy while he went up into the town and interviewed the house of Schiller, which he had not done yet; and as soon as he got himself away she came to business, breaking altogether from the inner drama with Miss Triscoe and devoting herself to Burnamy. They had already got so far as to have mentioned the meeting with the Triscoes in Wurzburg, and she said: "Did Mr. March tell you they were coming here? Or, no! We hadn't heard then. Yes, they are coming to-morrow. They may be going to stay some time. She talked of Weimar when we first spoke of Germany on the ship." Burnamy said nothing, and she suddenly added, with a sharp glance, "They wanted us to get them rooms, and we advised their coming to this house." He started very satisfactorily, and "Do you think they would be comfortable, here?" she pursued.

"Oh, yes, very. They can have my room; it's southeast; I shall be going into other quarters." She did not say anything; and "Mrs. March," he began again, "what is the use of my beating about the bush? You must know what I went back to Carlsbad for, that night—"

"No one ever told—"

"Well, you must have made a pretty good guess. But it was a failure. I ought to have failed, and I did. She said that unless her father liked it—And apparently he hasn't liked it." Burnamy smiled ruefully.

"How do you know? She didn't know where you were!"

"She could have got word to me if she had had good news for me. They've forwarded other letters from Pupp's. But it's all right; I had no business to go back to Carlsbad. Of course you didn't know I was in this house when you told them to come; and I must clear out. I had better clear out of Weimar, too."

"No, I don't think so; I have no right to pry into your affairs, but—"

"Oh, they're wide enough open!"

"And you may have changed your mind. I thought you might, when I saw you yesterday at Belvedere—"

"I was only trying to make bad worse."

"Then I think the situation has changed entirely through what Mr. Stoller said to Mr. March."

"I can't see how it has. I committed an act of shabby treachery, and I'm as much to blame as if he still wanted to punish me for it."

"Did Mr. March say that to you?"

"No; I said that to Mr. March; and he couldn't answer it, and you can't. You're very good, and very kind, but you can't answer it."

"I can answer it very well," she boasted, but she could find nothing better to say than, "It's your duty to her to see her and let her know."

"Doesn't she know already?"

"She has a right to know it from you. I think you are morbid, Mr. Burnamy. You know very well I didn't like your doing that to Mr. Stoller. I didn't say so at the time, because you seemed to feel it enough yourself. But I did like your owning up to it," and here Mrs. March thought it time to trot out her borrowed battle-horse again. "My husband always says that if a person owns up to an error, fully and faithfully, as you've always done, they make it the same in its consequences to them as if it had never been done."

"Does Mr. March say that?" asked Burnamy with a relenting smile.

"Indeed he does!"

Burnamy hesitated; then he asked, gloomily again:

"And what about the consequences to the, other fellow?"

"A woman," said Mrs. March, "has no concern with them. And besides, I think you've done all you could to save Mr. Stoller from the consequences."

"I haven't done anything."

"No matter. You would if you could. I wonder," she broke off, to prevent his persistence at a point where her nerves were beginning to give way, "what can be keeping Mr. March?"

Nothing much more important, it appeared later, than the pleasure of sauntering through the streets on the way to the house of Schiller, and looking at the pretty children going to school, with books under their arms. It was the day for the schools to open after the long summer vacation, and there was a freshness of expectation in the shining faces which, if it could not light up his own graybeard visage, could at least touch his heart:

When he reached the Schiller house he found that it was really not the Schiller house, but the Schiller flat, of three or four rooms, one flight up, whose windows look out upon the street named after the poet. The whole place is bare and clean; in one corner of the large room fronting the street stands Schiller's writing-table, with his chair before it; with the foot extending toward this there stands, in another corner, the narrow bed on which he died; some withered wreaths on the pillow frame a picture of his deathmask, which at first glance is like his dead face lying there. It is all rather tasteless, and all rather touching, and the place with its meagre appointments, as compared with the rich Goethe house, suggests that personal competition with Goethe in which Schiller is always falling into the second place. Whether it will be finally so with him in literature it is too early to ask of time, and upon other points eternity will not be interrogated. "The great, Goethe and the good Schiller," they remain; and yet, March reasoned, there was something good in Goethe and something great, in Schiller.

He was so full of the pathos of their inequality before the world that he did not heed the warning on the door of the pastry-shop near the Schiller house, and on opening it he bedaubed his hand with the fresh paint on it. He was then in such a state, that he could not bring his mind to bear upon the question of which cakes his wife would probably prefer, and he stood helplessly holding up his hand till the good woman behind the counter discovered his plight, and uttered a loud cry of compassion. She ran and got a wet napkin, which she rubbed with soap, and then she instructed him by word and gesture to rub his hand upon it, and she did not leave him till his rescue was complete. He let her choose a variety of the cakes for him, and came away with a gay paper bag full of them, and with the feeling that he had been in more intimate relations with the life of Weimar than travellers are often privileged to be. He argued from the instant and intelligent sympathy of the pastry woman a high grade of culture in all classes; and he conceived the notion of pretending to Mrs. March that he had got these cakes from, a descendant of Schiller.

His deceit availed with her for the brief moment in which she always, after so many years' experience of his duplicity, believed anything he told her. They dined merrily together at their hotel, and then Burnamy came down to the station with them and was very comfortable to March in helping him to get their tickets and their baggage registered. The train which was to take them to Halle, where they were to change for Berlin, was rather late, and they had but ten minutes after it came in before it would start again. Mrs. March was watching impatiently at the window of the waiting-room for the dismounting passengers to clear the platform and allow the doors to be opened; suddenly she gave a cry, and turned and ran into the passage by which the new arrivals were pouring out toward the superabundant omnibuses. March and Burnamy, who had been talking apart, mechanically rushed after her and found her kissing Miss Triscoe and shaking hands with the general amidst a tempest of questions and answers, from which it appeared that the Triscoes had got tired of staying in Wurzburg, and had simply come on to Weimar a day sooner than they had intended.

The, general was rather much bundled up for a day which was mild for a German summer day, and he coughed out an explanation that he had taken an abominable cold at that ridiculous parade, and had not shaken it off yet. He had a notion that change of air would be better for him; it could not be worse.

He seemed a little vague as to Burnamy, rather than inimical. While the ladies were still talking eagerly together in proffer and acceptance of Mrs. March's lamentations that she should be going away just as Miss Triscoe was coming, he asked if the omnibus for their hotel was there. He by no means resented Burnamy's assurance that it was, and he did not refuse to let him order their baggage, little and large, loaded upon it. By the time this was done, Mrs. March and Miss Triscoe had so far detached themselves from each other that they could separate after one more formal expression of regret and forgiveness. With a lament into which she poured a world of inarticulate emotions, Mrs. March wrenched herself from the place, and suffered herself, to be pushed toward her train. But with the last long look which she cast over her shoulder, before she vanished into the waiting-room, she saw Miss Triscoe and Burnamy transacting the elaborate politenesses of amiable strangers with regard to the very small bag which the girl had in her hand. He succeeded in relieving her of it; and then he led the way out of the station on the left of the general, while Miss Triscoe brought up the rear.

LXIII.

From the window of the train as it drew out Mrs. March tried for a glimpse of the omnibus in which her proteges were now rolling away together. As they were quite out of sight in the omnibus, which was itself out of sight, she failed, but as she fell back against her seat she treated the recent incident with a complexity and simultaneity of which no report can give an idea. At the end one fatal conviction remained: that in everything she had said she had failed to explain to Miss Triscoe how Burnamy happened to be in Weimar and how he happened to be there with them in the station. She required March to say how she had overlooked the very things which she ought to have mentioned first, and which she had on the point of her tongue the whole time. She went over the entire ground again to see if she could discover the reason why she had made such an unaccountable break, and it appeared that she was led to it by his rushing after her with Burnamy before she had had a chance to say a word about him; of course she could not say anything in his presence. This gave her some comfort, and there was consolation in the fact that she had left them together without the least intention or connivance, and now, no matter what happened, she could not accuse herself, and he could not accuse her of match-making.

He said that his own sense of guilt was so great that he should not dream of accusing her of anything except of regret that now she could never claim the credit of bringing the lovers together under circumstances so favorable. As soon as they were engaged they could join in renouncing her with a good conscience, and they would probably make this the basis of their efforts to propitiate the general.

She said she did not care, and with the mere removal of the lovers in space, her interest in them began to abate. They began to be of a minor importance in the anxieties of the change of trains at Halle, and in the excitement of settling into the express from Frankfort there were moments when they were altogether forgotten. The car was of almost American length, and it ran with almost American smoothness; when the conductor came and collected an extra fare for their seats, the Marches felt that if the charge had been two dollars instead of two marks they would have had every advantage of American travel.

On the way to Berlin the country was now fertile and flat, and now sterile and flat; near the capital the level sandy waste spread almost to its gates. The train ran quickly through the narrow fringe of suburbs, and then they were in one of those vast Continental stations which put our outdated depots to shame. The good 'traeger' who took possession of them and their hand-bags, put their boxes on a baggage-bearing drosky, and then got them another drosky for their personal transportation. This was a drosky of the first-class, but they would not have thought it so, either from the vehicle itself, or from the appearance of the driver and his horses. The public carriages of Germany are the shabbiest in the world; at Berlin the horses look like old hair trunks and the drivers like their moth-eaten contents.

The Marches got no splendor for the two prices they paid, and their approach to their hotel on Unter den Linden was as unimpressive as the ignoble avenue itself. It was a moist, cold evening, and the mean, tiresome street, slopped and splashed under its two rows of small trees, to which the thinning leaves clung like wet rags, between long lines of shops and hotels which had neither the grace of Paris nor the grandiosity of New York. March quoted in bitter derision:

"Bees, bees, was it your hydromel,
Under the Lindens?"

and his wife said that if Commonwealth Avenue in Boston could be imagined with its trees and without their beauty, flanked by the architecture of Sixth Avenue, with dashes of the west side of Union Square, that would be the famous Unter den Linden, where she had so resolutely decided that they would stay while in Berlin.

They had agreed upon the hotel, and neither could blame the other because it proved second-rate in everything but its charges. They ate a poorish table d'hote dinner in such low spirits that March had no heart to get a rise from his wife by calling her notice to the mouse which fed upon the crumbs about their feet while they dined. Their English-speaking waiter said that it was a very warm evening, and they never knew whether this was because he was a humorist, or because he was lonely and wished to talk, or because it really was a warm evening, for Berlin. When they had finished, they went out and drove about the greater part of the evening looking for another hotel, whose first requisite should be that it was not on Unter den Linden. What mainly determined Mrs. March in favor of the large, handsome, impersonal place they fixed upon was the fact that it was equipped for steam-heating; what determined March was the fact that it had a passenger-office where when he wished to leave, he could buy his railroad tickets and have his baggage checked without the maddening anxiety, of doing it at the station. But it was precisely in these points that the hotel which admirably fulfilled its other functions fell short. The weather made a succession of efforts throughout their stay to clear up cold; it merely grew colder without clearing up, but this seemed to offer no suggestion of steam for heating their bleak apartment and the chilly corridors to the management. With the help of a large lamp which they kept burning night and day they got the temperature of their rooms up to sixty; there was neither stove nor fireplace, the cold electric bulbs diffused a frosty glare; and in the vast, stately dining-room with its vaulted roof, there was nothing to warm them but their plates, and the handles of their knives and forks, which, by a mysterious inspiration, were always hot. When they were ready to go, March experienced from the apathy of the baggage clerk and the reluctance of the porters a more piercing distress than any he had known at the railroad stations; and one luckless valise which he ordered sent after him by express reached his bankers in Paris a fortnight overdue, with an accumulation of charges upon it outvaluing the books which it contained.

But these were minor defects in an establishment which had many merits, and was mainly of the temperament and intention of the large English railroad hotels. They looked from their windows down into a gardened square, peopled with a full share of the superabounding statues of Berlin and frequented by babies and nurse maids who seemed not to mind the cold any more than the stone kings and generals. The aspect of this square, like the excellent cooking of the hotel and the architecture of the imperial capital, suggested the superior civilization of Paris. Even the rows of gray houses and private palaces of Berlin are in the French taste, which is the only taste there is in Berlin. The suggestion of Paris is constant, but it is of Paris in exile, and without the chic which the city wears in its native air. The crowd lacks this as much as the architecture and the sculpture; there is no distinction among the men except for now and then a military figure, and among the women no style such as relieves the commonplace rash of the New York streets. The Berliners are plain and ill dressed, both men and women, and even the little children are plain. Every one is ill dressed, but no one is ragged, and among the undersized homely folk of the lower classes there is no such poverty-stricken shabbiness as shocks and insults the sight in New York. That which distinctly recalls our metropolis is the lofty passage of the elevated trains intersecting the prospectives of many streets; but in Berlin the elevated road is carried on massive brick archways and not lifted upon gay, crazy iron ladders like ours.

When you look away from this, and regard Berlin on its aesthetic, side you are again in that banished Paris, whose captive art-soul is made to serve, so far as it may be enslaved to such an effect, in the celebration of the German triumph over France. Berlin has never the presence of a great capital, however, in spite of its perpetual monumental insistence. There is no streaming movement in broad vistas; the dull looking population moves sluggishly; there is no show of fine equipages. The prevailing tone of the city and the sky is gray; but under the cloudy heaven there is no responsive Gothic solemnity in the architecture. There are hints of the older German cities in some of the remote and observe streets, but otherwise all is as new as Boston, which in fact the actual Berlin hardly antedates.

There are easily more statues in Berlin than in any other city in the world, but they only unite in failing to give Berlin an artistic air. They stand in long rows on the cornices; they crowd the pediments; they poise on one leg above domes and arches; they shelter themselves in niches; they ride about on horseback; they sit or lounge on street corners or in garden walks; all with a mediocrity in the older sort which fails of any impression. If they were only furiously baroque they would be something, and it may be from a sense of this that there is a self-assertion in the recent sculptures, which are always patriotic, more noisy and bragging than anything else in perennial brass. This offensive art is the modern Prussian avatar of the old German romantic spirit, and bears the same relation to it that modern romanticism in literature bears to romance. It finds its apotheosis in the monument to Kaiser Wilhelm I., a vast incoherent group of swelling and swaggering bronze, commemorating the victory of the first Prussian Emperor in the war with the last French Emperor, and avenging the vanquished upon the victors by its ugliness. The ungainly and irrelevant assemblage of men and animals backs away from the imperial palace, and saves itself too soon from plunging over the border of a canal behind it, not far from Rauch's great statue of the great Frederic. To come to it from the simplicity and quiet of that noble work is like passing from some exquisite masterpiece of naturalistic acting to the rant and uproar of melodrama; and the Marches stood stunned and bewildered by its wild explosions.

When they could escape they found themselves so convenient to the imperial palace that they judged best to discharge at once the obligation to visit it which must otherwise weigh upon them. They entered the court without opposition from the sentinel, and joined other strangers straggling instinctively toward a waiting-room in one corner of the building, where after they had increased to some thirty, a custodian took charge of them, and led them up a series of inclined plains of brick to the state apartments. In the antechamber they found a provision of immense felt over-shoes which they were expected to put on for their passage over the waxed marquetry of the halls. These roomy slippers were designed for the accommodation of the native boots; and upon the mixed company of foreigners the effect was in the last degree humiliating. The women's skirts some what hid their disgrace, but the men were openly put to shame, and they shuffled forward with their bodies at a convenient incline like a company of snow-shoers. In the depths of his own abasement March heard a female voice behind him sighing in American accents, "To think I should be polishing up these imperial floors with my republican feet!"

The protest expressed the rebellion which he felt mounting in his own heart as they advanced through the heavily splendid rooms, in the historical order of the family portraits recording the rise of the Prussian sovereigns from

Margraves to Emperors. He began to realize here the fact which grew open him more and more that imperial Germany is not the effect of a popular impulse but of a dynastic propensity. There is nothing original in the imperial palace, nothing national; it embodies and proclaims a powerful personal will, and in its adaptations of French art it appeals to no emotion in the German witness nobler than his pride in the German triumph over the French in war. March found it tiresome beyond the tiresome wont of palaces, and he gladly shook off the sense of it with his felt shoes. "Well," he confided to his wife when they were fairly out-of-doors, "if Prussia rose in the strength of silence, as Carlyle wants us to believe, she is taking it out in talk now, and tall talk."

"Yes, isn't she!" Mrs. March assented, and with a passionate desire for excess in a bad thing, which we all know at times, she looked eagerly about her for proofs of that odious militarism of the empire, which ought to have been conspicuous in the imperial capital; but possibly because the troops were nearly all away at the manoeuvres, there were hardly more in the streets than she had sometimes seen in Washington. Again the German officers signally failed to offer her any rudeness when she met them on the side-walks. There were scarcely any of them, and perhaps that might have been the reason why they were not more aggressive; but a whole company of soldiers marching carelessly up to the palace from the Brandenburg gate, without music, or so much style as our own militia often puts on, regarded her with inoffensive eyes so far as they looked at her. She declared that personally there was nothing against the Prussians; even when in uniform they were kindly and modest-looking men; it was when they got up on pedestals, in bronze or marble, that they, began to bully and to brag.

LXIV.

The dinner which the Marches got at a restaurant on Unter den Linden almost redeemed the avenue from the disgrace it had fallen into with them. It was, the best meal they had yet eaten in Europe, and as to fact and form was a sort of compromise between a French dinner and an English dinner which they did not hesitate to pronounce Prussian. The waiter who served it was a friendly spirit, very sensible of their intelligent appreciation of the dinner; and from him they formed a more respectful opinion of Berlin civilization than they had yet held. After the manner of strangers everywhere they judged the country they were visiting from such of its inhabitants as chance brought them in contact with; and it would really be a good thing for nations that wish to stand well with the world at large to look carefully to the behavior of its cabmen and car conductors, its hotel clerks and waiters, its theatre-ticket sellers and ushers, its policemen and sacristans, its landlords and salesmen; for by these rather than by its society women and its statesmen and divines, is it really judged in the books of travellers; some attention also should be paid to the weather, if the climate is to be praised. In the railroad cafe at Potsdam there was a waiter so rude to the Marches that if they had not been people of great strength of character he would have undone the favorable impression the soldiers and civilians of Berlin generally had been at such pains to produce in them; and throughout the week of early September which they passed there, it rained so much and so bitterly, it was so wet and so cold, that they might have come away thinking it's the worst climate in the world, if it had not been for a man whom they saw in one of the public gardens pouring a heavy stream from his garden hose upon the shrubbery already soaked and shuddering in the cold. But this convinced them that they were suffering from weather and not from the climate, which must really be hot and dry; and they went home to their hotel and sat contentedly down in a temperature of sixty degrees. The weather, was not always so bad; one day it was dry cold instead of wet cold, with rough, rusty clouds breaking a blue sky; another day, up to eleven in the forenoon, it was like Indian summer; then it changed to a harsh November air; and then it relented and ended so mildly, that they hired chairs in the place before the imperial palace for five pfennigs each, and sat watching the life before them. Motherly women-folk were there knitting; two American girls in chairs near them chatted together; some fine equipages, the only ones they saw in Berlin, went by; a dog and a man (the wife who ought to have been in harness was probably sick, and the poor fellow was forced to take her place) passed dragging a cart; some schoolboys who had hung their satchels upon the low railing were playing about the base of the statue of King William III. in the joyous freedom of German childhood.

They seemed the gayer for the brief moments of sunshine, but to the Americans, who were Southern by virtue of their sky, the brightness had a sense of lurking winter in it, such as they remembered feeling on a sunny day in Quebec. The blue heaven looked sad; but they agreed that it fitly roofed the bit of old feudal Berlin which forms the most ancient wing of the Schloss. This was time-blackened and rude, but at least it did not try to be French, and it overhung the Spree which winds through the city and gives it the greatest charm it has. In fact Berlin, which is otherwise so grandiose without grandeur and so severe without impressiveness, is sympathetic wherever the Spree opens it to the sky. The stream is spanned by many bridges, and bridges cannot well be unpicturesque, especially if they have statues to help them out. The Spree abounds in bridges, and it has a charming habit of slow hay-laden barges; at the landings of the little passenger-steamers which ply upon it there are cafes and summer-gardens, and these even in the inclement air of September suggested a friendly gayety.

The Marches saw it best in the tour of the elevated road in Berlin which they made in an impassioned memory of the elevated road in New York. The brick viaducts which carry this arch the Spree again and again in their course through and around the city, but with never quite such spectacular effects as our spidery tressels, achieve. The stations are pleasant, sometimes with lunch-counters and news-stands, but have not the comic-opera-chalet prettiness of ours, and are not so frequent. The road is not so smooth, the cars not so smooth-running or so swift. On the other hand they are comfortably cushioned, and they are never overcrowded. The line is at times above, at times below the houses, and at times on a level with them, alike in city and in suburbs. The train whirled out of thickly built districts, past the backs of the old houses, into outskirts thinly populated, with new houses springing up without order or continuity among the meadows and vegetable-gardens, and along the ready-made, elm-planted avenues, where wooden fences divided the vacant lots. Everywhere the city was growing out over the country, in blocks and detached edifices of limestone, sandstone, red and yellow brick, larger or smaller, of no more uniformity than our suburban dwellings, but never of their ugliness or lawless offensiveness.

In an effort for the intimate life of the country March went two successive mornings for his breakfast to the Cafe Bauer, which has some admirable wall-printings, and is the chief cafe on Unter den Linden; but on both days there were more people in the paintings than out of them. The second morning the waiter who took his order recognized him and asked, "Wie gestern?" and from this he argued an affectionate constancy in the Berliners, and a hospitable observance of the tastes of strangers. At his bankers, on the other hand, the cashier scrutinized his signature and remarked that it did not look like the signature in his letter of credit, and then he inferred a suspicious mind in the moneyed classes of Prussia; as he had not been treated with such unkind doubt by Hebrew bankers anywhere, he made a mental note that the Jews were politer than the Christians in Germany. In starting for Potsdam he asked a traeger where the Potsdam train was and the man said, "Dat train dare," and in coming back he helped a fat old lady out of the car, and she thanked him in English. From these incidents, both occurring the same day in the same place, the inference of a widespread knowledge of our language in all classes of the population was inevitable.

In this obvious and easy manner he studied contemporary civilization in the capital. He even carried his researches farther, and went one rainy afternoon to an exhibition of modern pictures in a pavilion of the Thiergarten, where from the small attendance he inferred an indifference to the arts which he would not ascribe to the weather. One evening at a summer theatre where they gave the pantomime of the 'Puppenfee' and the operetta of 'Hansel and Gretel', he observed that the greater part of the audience was composed of nice plain young girls and children, and he noted that there was no sort of evening dress; from the large number of Americans present he imagined a numerous colony in Berlin, where they mast have an instinctive sense of their co-nationality, since one of them in the stress of getting his hat and overcoat when they all came out, confidently addressed him in English. But he took stock of his impressions with his wife, and they seemed to him so few, after all, that he could not resist a painful sense of isolation in the midst of the environment.

They made a Sunday excursion to the Zoological Gardens in the Thiergarten, with a large crowd of the lower classes, but though they had a great deal of trouble in getting there by the various kinds of horsecars and electric cars, they did not feel that they had got near to the popular life. They endeavored for some sense of Berlin society by driving home in a drosky, and on the way they passed rows of beautiful houses, in French and Italian taste, fronting the deep, damp green park from the Thiergartenstrasse, in which they were confident cultivated and delightful people lived; but they remained to the last with nothing but their unsupported conjecture.

LXV.

Their excursion to Potsdam was the cream of their sojourn in Berlin. They chose for it the first fair morning, and they ran out over the flat sandy plains surrounding the capital, and among the low hills surrounding Potsdam before it actually began to rain.

They wished immediately to see Sans Souci for the great Frederick's sake, and they drove through a lively shower to the palace, where they waited with a horde of twenty-five other tourists in a gusty colonnade before they were led through Voltaire's room and Frederick's death chamber.

The French philosopher comes before the Prussian prince at Sans Souci even in the palatial villa which expresses the wilful caprice of the great Frederick as few edifices have embodied the whims or tastes of their owners. The whole affair is eighteenth-century French, as the Germans conceived it. The gardened terrace from which the low, one-story building, thickly crusted with baroque sculptures, looks down into a many-colored parterre, was luxuriantly French, and sentimentally French the colonnaded front opening to a perspective of artificial ruins, with broken pillars lifting a conscious fragment of architrave against the sky. Within, all again was French in the design, the decoration and the furnishing. At that time there, was in fact no other taste, and Frederick, who despised and disused his native tongue, was resolved upon French taste even in his intimate companionship. The droll story of his coquetry with the terrible free spirit which he got from France to be his guest is vividly reanimated at Sans Souci, where one breathes the very air in which the strangely assorted companions lived, and in which they parted so soon to pursue each other with brutal annoyance on one side, and with merciless mockery on the other. Voltaire was long ago revenged upon his host for all the indignities he suffered from him in their comedy; he left deeply graven upon Frederick's fame the trace of those lacerating talons which he could strike to the quick; and it is the singular effect of this scene of their brief friendship that one feels there the pre-eminence of the wit in whatever was most important to mankind.

The rain had lifted a little and the sun shone out on the bloom of the lovely parterre where the Marches profited by a smiling moment to wander among the statues and the roses heavy with the shower. Then they walked back to their carriage and drove to the New Palace, which expresses in differing architectural terms the same subjection to an alien ideal of beauty. It is thronged without by delightfully preposterous rococo statues, and within it is rich in all those curiosities and memorials of royalty with which palaces so well know how to fatigue the flesh and spirit of their visitors.

The Marches escaped from it all with sighs and groans of relief, and before they drove off to see the great fountain of the Orangeries, they dedicated a moment of pathos to the Temple of Friendship which Frederick built in memory of unhappy Wilhelmina of Beyreuth, the sister he loved in the common sorrow of their wretched home, and neglected when he came to his kingdom. It is beautiful in its rococo way, swept up to on its terrace by most noble staircases, and swaggered over by baroque allegories of all sorts: Everywhere the statues outnumbered the visitors, who may have been kept away by the rain; the statues naturally did not mind it.

Sometime in the midst of their sight-seeing the Marches had dinner in a mildewed restaurant, where a compatriotic accent caught their ear in a voice saying to the waiter, "We are in a hurry." They looked round and saw that it proceeded from the pretty nose of a young American girl, who sat with a party of young American girls at a neighboring table. Then they perceived that all the people in that restaurant were Americans, mostly young girls, who all looked as if they were in a hurry. But neither their beauty nor their impatience had the least effect with the waiter, who prolonged the dinner at his pleasure, and alarmed the Marches with the misgiving that they should not have time for the final palace on their list.

This was the palace where the father of Frederick, the mad old Frederick William, brought up his children with that severity which Solomon urged but probably did not practise. It is a vast place, but they had time for it all, though the custodian made the most of them as the latest comers of the day, and led them through it with a prolixity as great as their waiter's. He was a most friendly custodian, and when he found that they had some little notion of what they wanted to see, he mixed zeal with his patronage, and in a manner made them his honored guests. They saw everything but the doorway where the faithful royal father used to lie in wait for his children and beat them, princes and princesses alike, with his knobby cane as they came through. They might have seen this doorway without knowing it; but from the window overlooking the parade-ground where his family watched the manoeuvres of his gigantic grenadiers, they made sure of just such puddles as Frederick William forced his family to sit with their feet in, while they dined alfresco on pork and cabbage; and they visited the room of the Smoking Parliament where he ruled his convives with a rod of iron, and made them the victims of his bad jokes. The measuring-board against which he took the stature of his tall grenadiers is there, and one room is devoted to those masterpieces which he used to paint in the agonies of gout. His chef d'oeuvre contains a figure with two left feet, and there seemed no reason why it might not have had three. In another room is a small statue of Carlyle, who did so much to rehabilitate the house which the daughter of it, Wilhelmina, did so much to demolish in the regard of men.

The palace is now mostly kept for guests, and there is a chamber where Napoleon slept, which is not likely to be occupied soon by any other self-invited guest of his nation. It is perhaps to keep the princes of Europe humble that hardly a palace on the Continent is without the chamber of this adventurer, who, till he stooped to be like them, was easily their master. Another democracy had here recorded its invasion in the American stoves which the custodian pointed out in the corridor when Mrs, March, with as little delay as possible, had proclaimed their country. The custodian professed an added respect for them from the fact, and if he did not feel it, no doubt he merited the drink money which they lavished on him at parting.

Their driver also was a congenial spirit, and when he let them out of his carriage at the station, he excused the rainy day to them. He was a merry fellow beyond the wont of his nation, and he-laughed at the bad weather, as if it had been a good joke on them.

His gayety, and the red sunset light, which shone on the stems of the pines on the way back to Berlin, contributed to the content in which they reviewed their visit to Potsdam. They agreed that the place was perfectly charming, and that it was incomparably expressive of kingly will and pride. These had done there on the grand scale what all the German princes and princelings had tried to do in imitation and emulation of French splendor. In Potsdam the grandeur, was not a historical growth as at Versailles, but was the effect of family genius, in which there was often the curious fascination of insanity.

They felt this strongly again amidst the futile monuments of the Hohenzollern Museum, in Berlin, where all the portraits, effigies, personal belongings and memorials of that gifted, eccentric race are gathered and historically disposed. The princes of the mighty line who stand out from the rest are Frederick the Great and his infuriate. father; and in the waxen likeness of the son, a small thin figure, terribly spry, and a face pitilessly alert, appears something of the madness which showed in the life of the sire.

They went through many rooms in which the memorials of the kings and queens, the emperors and empresses were carefully ordered, and felt no kindness except before the relics relating to the Emperor Frederick and his mother. In the presence of the greatest of the dynasty they experienced a kind of terror which March expressed, when they were safely away, in the confession of his joy that those people were dead.

LXVI.

The rough weather which made Berlin almost uninhabitable to Mrs. March had such an effect with General Triscoe at Weimar that under the orders of an English-speaking doctor he retreated from it altogether and went to bed. Here he escaped the bronchitis which had attacked him, and his convalesence left him so little to complain of that he could not always keep his temper. In the absence of actual offence, either from his daughter or from Burnamy, his sense of injury took a retroactive form; it centred first in Stoller and the twins; then it diverged toward Rose Adding, his mother and Kenby, and finally involved the Marches in the same measure of inculpation; for they had each and all had part, directly or indirectly, in the chances that brought on his cold.

He owed to Burnamy the comfort of the best room in the hotel, and he was constantly dependent upon his kindness; but he made it evident that he did not over-value Burnamy's sacrifice and devotion, and that it was not an unmixed pleasure, however great a convenience, to have him about. In giving up his room, Burnamy had proposed going out of the hotel altogether; but General Triscoe heard of this with almost as great vexation as he had accepted the room. He besought him not to go, but so ungraciously that his daughter was ashamed, and tried to atone for his manner by the kindness of her own.

Perhaps General Triscoe would not have been without excuse if he were not eager to have her share with destitute merit the fortune which she had hitherto shared only with him. He was old, and certain luxuries had become habits if not necessaries with him. Of course he did not say this to himself; and still less did he say it to her. But he let her see that he did not enjoy the chance which had thrown them again in such close relations with Burnamy, and he did pot hide his belief that the Marches were somehow to blame for it. This made it impossible for her to write at once to Mrs. March as she had promised; but she was determined that it should not make her unjust to Burnamy. She would not avoid him; she would not let anything that had happened keep her from showing that she felt his kindness and was glad of his help.

Of course they knew no one else in Weimar, and his presence merely as a fellow-countryman would have been precious. He got them a doctor, against General Triscoe's will; he went for his medicines; he lent him books and papers; he sat with him and tried to amuse him. But with the girl he attempted no return to the situation at Carlsbad; there is nothing like the delicate pride of a young man who resolves to forego unfair advantage in love.

The day after their arrival, when her father was making up for the sleep he had lost by night, she found herself alone in the little reading-room of the hotel with Burnamy for the first time, and she said: "I suppose you must have been all over Weimar by this time."

"Well, I've been here, off and on, almost a month. It's an interesting place. There's a good deal of the old literary quality left."

"And you enjoy that! I saw"—she added this with a little unnecessary flush—"your poem in the paper you lent papa."

"I suppose I ought to have kept that back. But I couldn't." He laughed, and she said:

"You must find a great deal of inspiration in such a literary place."

"It isn't lying about loose, exactly." Even in the serious and perplexing situation in which he found himself he could not help being amused with her unliterary notions of literature, her conventional and commonplace conceptions of it. They had their value with him as those of a more fashionable world than his own, which he believed was somehow a greater world. At the same time he believed that she was now interposing them between the present and the past, and forbidding with them any return to the mood of their last meeting in Carlsbad. He looked at her ladylike composure and unconsciousness, and wondered if she could be the same person and the same person as they who lost themselves in the crowd that night and heard and said words palpitant with fate. Perhaps there had been no such words; perhaps it was all a hallucination. He must leave her to recognize that it was reality; till she did so, he felt bitterly that there was nothing for him but submission and patience; if she never did so, there was nothing for him but acquiescence.

In this talk and in the talks they had afterwards she seemed willing enough to speak of what had happened since: of coming on to Wurzburg with the Addings and of finding the Marches there; of Rose's collapse, and of his mother's flight seaward with him in the care of Kenby, who was so fortunately going to Holland, too. He on his side told her of going to Wurzburg for the manoeuvres, and they agreed that it was very strange they had not met.

She did not try to keep their relations from taking the domestic character which was inevitable, and it seemed to him that this in itself was significant of a determination on her part that was fatal to his hopes. With a lover's indefinite power of blinding himself to what is before his eyes, he believed that if she had been more diffident of him, more uneasy in his presence, he should have had more courage; but for her to breakfast unafraid with him, to meet him at lunch and dinner in the little dining-room where they were often the only guests, and always the only English-speaking guests, was nothing less than prohibitive.

In the hotel service there was one of those men who are porters in this world, but will be angels in the next, unless the perfect goodness of their looks, the constant kindness of their acts, belies them. The Marches had known and loved the man in their brief stay, and he had been the fast friend of Burnamy from the moment they first saw each other at the station. He had tenderly taken possession of General Triscoe on his arrival, and had constituted himself the nurse and keeper of the irascible invalid, in the intervals of going to the trains, with a zeal that often relieved his daughter and Burnamy. The general in fact preferred him to either, and a tacit custom grew up by which when August knocked at his door, and offered himself in his few words of serviceable English, that one of them who happened to be sitting with the general gave way, and left him in charge. The retiring watcher was then apt to encounter the other watcher on the stairs, or in the reading-room, or in the tiny, white-pebbled door-yard at a little table in the shade of the wooden-tubbed evergreens. From the habit of doing this they one day suddenly formed the habit of going across the street to that gardened hollow before and below the Grand-Ducal Museum. There was here a bench in the shelter of some late-flowering bush which the few other frequenters of the place soon recognized as belonging to the young strangers, so that they would silently rise and leave it to them when they saw them coming. Apparently they yielded not only to their right, but to a certain authority which resides in lovers, and which all other men, and especially all other women, like to acknowledge and respect.

In the absence of any civic documents bearing upon the affair it is difficult to establish the fact that this was the character in which Agatha and Burnamy were commonly regarded by the inhabitants of Weimar. But whatever their own notion of their relation was, if it was not that of a Brant and a Brautigam, the people of Weimar would have been puzzled to say what it was. It was known that the gracious young lady's father, who would naturally have accompanied them, was sick, and in the fact that they were Americans much extenuation was found for whatever was phenomenal in their unencumbered enjoyment of each other's society.

If their free American association was indistinguishably like the peasant informality which General Triscoe despised in the relations of Kenby and Mrs. Adding, it is to be said in his excuse that he could not be fully cognizant of it, in the circumstances, and so could do nothing to prevent it. His pessimism extended to his health; from the first he believed himself worse than the doctor thought him, and he would have had some other physician if he had not found consolation in their difference of opinion and the consequent contempt which he was enabled to cherish for the doctor in view of the man's complete ignorance of the case. In proof of his own better understanding of it, he remained in bed some time after the doctor said he might get up.

Nearly ten days had passed before he left his room, and it was not till then that he clearly saw how far affairs had gone with his daughter and Burnamy, though even then his observance seemed to have anticipated theirs. He found them in a quiet acceptance of the fortune which had brought them together, so contented that they appeared to ask nothing more of it. The divine patience and confidence of their youth might sometimes have had almost the effect of indifference to a witness who had seen its evolution from the moods of the first few days of their reunion in Weimar. To General Triscoe, however, it looked like an understanding which had been made without reference to his wishes, and had not been directly brought to his knowledge.

"Agatha," he said, after due note of a gay contest between her and Burnamy over the pleasure and privilege of ordering his supper sent to his room when he had gone back to it from his first afternoon in the open air, "how long is that young man going to stay in Weimar?"

"Why, I don't know!" she answered, startled from her work of beating the sofa pillows into shape, and pausing with one of them in her hand. "I never asked him." She looked down candidly into his face where he sat in an easy-chair waiting for her arrangement of the sofa. "What makes you ask?"

He answered with another question. "Does he know that we had thought of staying here?"

"Why, we've always talked of that, haven't we? Yes, he knows it. Didn't you want him to know it, papa? You ought to have begun on the ship, then. Of course I've asked him what sort of place it was. I'm sorry if you didn't want me to."

"Have I said that? It's perfectly easy to push on to Paris. Unless—"

"Unless what?" Agatha dropped the pillow, and listened respectfully. But in spite of her filial attitude she could not keep her youth and strength and courage from quelling the forces of the elderly man.

He said querulously, "I don't see why you take that tone with me. You certainly know what I mean. But if you don't care to deal openly with me, I won't ask you." He dropped his eyes from her face, and at the same time a deep blush began to tinge it, growing up from her neck to her forehead. "You must know—you're not a child," he continued, still with averted eyes, "that this sort of thing can't go on... It must be something else, or it mustn't be anything at all. I don't ask you for your confidence, and you know that I've never sought to control you."

This was not the least true, but Agatha answered, either absently or provisionally, "No."

"And I don't seek to do so now. If you have nothing that you wish to tell me—"

He waited, and after what seemed a long time, she asked as if she had not heard him, "Will you lie down a little before your supper, papa?"

"I will lie down when I feel like it," he answered. "Send August with the supper; he can look after me."

His resentful tone, even more than his words, dismissed her, but she left him without apparent grievance, saying quietly, "I will send August."

LXVII.

Agatha did not come down to supper with Burnamy. She asked August, when she gave him her father's order, to have a cup of tea sent to her room, where, when it came, she remained thinking so long that it was rather tepid by the time she drank it.

Then she went to her window, and looked out, first above and next below. Above, the moon was hanging over the gardened hollow before the Museum with the airy lightness of an American moon. Below was Burnamy behind the tubbed evergreens, sitting tilted in his chair against the house wall, with the spark of his cigar fainting and flashing like an American firefly. Agatha went down to the door, after a little delay, and seemed surprised to find him there; at least she said, "Oh!" in a tone of surprise.

Burnamy stood up, and answered, "Nice night."

"Beautiful!" she breathed. "I didn't suppose the sky in Germany could ever be so clear."

"It seems to be doing its best."

"The flowers over there look like ghosts in the light," she said dreamily.

"They're not. Don't you want to get your hat and wrap, and go over and expose the fraud?"

"Oh," she answered, as if it were merely a question of the hat and wrap, "I have them."

They sauntered through the garden walks for a while, long enough to have ascertained that there was not a veridical phantom among the flowers, if they had been looking, and then when they came to their accustomed seat, they sat down, and she said, "I don't know that I've seen the moon so clear since we left Carlsbad." At the last word his heart gave a jump that seemed to lodge it in his throat and kept him from speaking, so that she could resume without interruption, "I've got something of yours, that you left at the Posthof. The girl that broke the dishes found it, and Lili gave it to Mrs. March for you." This did not account for Agatha's having the thing, whatever it was; but when she took a handkerchief from her belt, and put out her hand with it toward him, he seemed to find that her having it had necessarily followed. He tried to take it from her, but his own hand trembled so that it clung to hers, and he gasped, "Can't you say now, what you wouldn't say then?"

The logical sequence was no more obvious than before; but she apparently felt it in her turn as he had felt it in his. She whispered back, "Yes," and then she could not get out anything more till she entreated in a half-stifled voice, "Oh, don't!"

"No, no!" he panted. "I won't—I oughtn't to have done it—I beg your pardon—I oughtn't to have spoken,—even—I—"

She returned in a far less breathless and tremulous fashion, but still between laughing and crying, "I meant to make you. And now, if you're ever sorry, or I'm ever too topping about anything, you can be perfectly free to say that you'd never have spoken if you hadn't seen that I wanted you to."

"But I didn't see any such thing," he protested. "I spoke because I couldn't help it any longer."

She laughed triumphantly. "Of course you think so! And that shows that you are only a man after all; in spite of your finessing. But I am going to have the credit of it. I knew that you were holding back because you were too proud, or thought you hadn't the right, or something. Weren't you?" She startled him with the sudden vehemence of her challenge: "If you pretend, that you weren't I shall never forgive you!"

"But I was! Of course I was. I was afraid—"

"Isn't that what I said?" She triumphed over him with another laugh, and cowered a little closer to him, if that could be.

They were standing, without knowing how they had got to their feet; and now without any purpose of the kind, they began to stroll again among the garden paths, and to ask and to answer questions, which touched every point of their common history, and yet left it a mine of inexhaustible knowledge for all future time. Out of the sweet and dear delight of this encyclopedian reserve two or three facts appeared with a present distinctness. One of these was that Burnamy had regarded her refusal to be definite at Carlsbad as definite refusal, and had meant never to see her again, and certainly never to speak again of love to her. Another point was that she had not resented his coming back that last night, but had been proud and happy in it as proof of his love, and had always meant somehow to let him know that she was torched by his trusting her enough to come back while he was still under that cloud with Mr. Stoller. With further logic, purely of the heart, she acquitted him altogether of wrong in that affair, and alleged in proof, what Mr. Stoller had said of it to Mr. March. Burnamy owned that he knew what Stoller had said, but even in his present condition he could not accept fully her reading of that obscure passage of his life. He preferred to put the question by, and perhaps neither of them cared anything about it except as it related to the fact that they were now each other's forever.

They agreed that they must write to Mr. and Mrs. March at once; or at least, Agatha said, as soon as she had spoken to her father. At her mention of her father she was aware of a doubt, a fear, in Burnamy which expressed itself by scarcely more than a spiritual consciousness from his arm to the hands which she had clasped within it. "He has always appreciated you," she said courageously, "and I know he will see it in the right light."

She probably meant no more than to affirm her faith in her own ability finally to bring her father to a just mind concerning it; but Burnamy accepted her assurance with buoyant hopefulness, and said he would see General Triscoe the first thing in the morning.

"No, I will see him," she said, "I wish to see him first; he will expect it of me. We had better go in, now," she added, but neither made any motion for the present to do so. On the contrary, they walked in the other direction, and it was an hour after Agatha declared their duty in the matter before they tried to fulfil it.

Then, indeed, after they returned to the hotel, she lost no time in going to her father beyond that which must be given to a long hand-pressure under the fresco of the five poets on the stairs landing, where her ways and Burnamy's parted. She went into her own room, and softly opened the door into her father's and listened.

"Well?" he said in a sort of challenging voice.

"Have you been asleep?" she asked.

"I've just blown out my light. What has kept you?"

She did not reply categorically. Standing there in the sheltering dark, she said, "Papa, I wasn't very candid with you, this afternoon. I am engaged to Mr. Burnamy."

"Light the candle," said her father. "Or no," he added before she could do so. "Is it quite settled?"

"Quite," she answered in a voice that admitted of no doubt. "That is, as far as it can be, without you."

"Don't be a hypocrite, Agatha," said the general. "And let me try to get to sleep. You know I don't like it, and you know I can't help it."

"Yes," the girl assented.

"Then go to bed," said the general concisely.

Agatha did not obey her father. She thought she ought to kiss him, but she decided that she had better postpone this; so she merely gave him a tender goodnight, to which he made no response, and shut herself into her own room, where she remained sitting and staring out into the moonlight, with a smile that never left her lips.

When the moon sank below the horizon, the sky was pale with the coming day, but before it was fairly dawn, she saw something white, not much greater than some moths, moving before her window. She pulled the valves open and found it a bit of paper attached to a thread dangling from above. She broke it loose and in the morning twilight she read the great central truth of the universe:

"I love you. L. J. B."

She wrote under the tremendous inspiration:

"So do I. Don't be silly. A. T."

She fastened the paper to the thread again, and gave it a little twitch. She waited for the low note of laughter which did not fail to flutter down from above; then she threw herself upon the bed, and fell asleep.

It was not so late as she thought when she woke, and it seemed, at breakfast, that Burnamy had been up still earlier. Of the three involved in the anxiety of the night before General Triscoe was still respited from it by sleep, but he woke much more haggard than either of the young people. They, in fact, were not at all haggard; the worst was over, if bringing their engagement to his knowledge was the worst; the formality of asking his consent which Burnamy still had to go through was unpleasant, but after all it was a formality. Agatha told him everything that had passed between herself and her father, and if it had not that cordiality on his part which they could have wished it was certainly not hopelessly discouraging.

They agreed at breakfast that Burnamy had better have it over as quickly as possible, and he waited only till August came down with the general's tray before going up to his room. The young fellow did not feel more at his ease than the elder meant he should in taking the chair to which the general waved him from where he lay in bed; and there was no talk wasted upon the weather between them.

"I suppose I know what you have come for, Mr. Burnamy," said General Triscoe in a tone which was rather judicial than otherwise, "and I suppose you know why you have come." The words certainly opened the way for Burnamy, but he hesitated so long to take it that the general had abundant time to add, "I don't pretend that this event is unexpected, but I should like to know what reason you have for thinking I should wish you to marry my daughter. I take it for granted that you are attached to each other, and we won't waste time on that point. Not to beat about the bush, on the next point, let me ask at once what your means of supporting her are. How much did you earn on that newspaper in Chicago?"

"Fifteen hundred dollars," Burnamy answered, promptly enough.

"Did you earn anything more, say within the last year?"

"I got three hundred dollars advance copyright for a book I sold to a publisher." The glory had not yet faded from the fact in Burnamy's mind.

"Eighteen hundred. What did you get for your poem in March's book?"

"That's a very trifling matter: fifteen dollars."

"And your salary as private secretary to that man Stoller?"

"Thirty dollars a week, and my expenses. But I wouldn't take that, General Triscoe," said Burnamy.

General Triscoe, from his 'lit de justice', passed this point in silence. "Have you any one dependent on you?"

"My mother; I take care of my mother," answered Burnamy, proudly.

"Since you have broken with Stoller, what are your prospects?"

"I have none."

"Then you don't expect to support my daughter; you expect to live upon her means."

"I expect to do nothing of the kind!" cried Burnamy. "I should be ashamed— I should feel disgraced—I should—I don't ask you—I don't ask her till I have the means to support her—"

"If you were very fortunate," continued the general, unmoved by the young fellow's pain, and unperturbed by the fact that he had himself lived upon his wife's means as long as she lived, and then upon his daughter's, "if you went back to Stoller—"

"I wouldn't go back to him. I don't say he's knowingly a rascal, but he's ignorantly a rascal, and he proposed a rascally thing to me. I behaved badly to him, and I'd give anything to undo the wrong I let him do himself; but I'll never go back to him."

"If you went back, on your old salary," the general persisted pitilessly, "you would be very fortunate if you brought your earnings up to twenty-five hundred a year."

"Yes—"

"And how far do you think that would go in supporting my daughter on the scale she is used to? I don't speak of your mother, who has the first claim upon you."

Burnamy sat dumb; and his head which he had lifted indignantly when the question was of Stoller, began to sink.

The general went on. "You ask me to give you my daughter when you haven't money enough to keep her in gowns; you ask me to give her to a stranger—"

"Not quite a stranger, General Triscoe," Burnamy protested. "You have known me for three months at least, and any one who knows me in Chicago will tell you—"

"A stranger, and worse than a stranger," the general continued, so pleased with the logical perfection of his position that he almost smiled, and certainly softened toward Burnamy. "It isn't a question of liking you, Mr. Burnamy, but of knowing you; my daughter likes you; so do the Marches; so does everybody who has met you. I like you myself. You've done me personally a thousand kindnesses. But I know very little of you, in spite of our three months' acquaintance; and that little is—But you shall judge for yourself! You were in the confidential employ of a man who trusted you, and you let him betray himself."

"I did. I don't excuse it. The thought of it burns like fire. But it wasn't done maliciously; it wasn't done falsely; it was done inconsiderately; and when it was done, it seemed irrevocable. But it wasn't; I could have prevented, I could have stooped the mischief; and I didn't! I can never outlive that."

"I know," said the general relentlessly, "that you have never attempted any defence. That has been to your credit with me. It inclined me to overlook your unwarranted course in writing to my daughter, when you told her you would never see her again. What did you expect me to think, after that, of your coming back to see her? Or didn't you expect me to know it?"

"I expected you to know it; I knew she would tell you. But I don't excuse that, either. It was acting a lie to come back. All I can say is that I had to see her again for one last time."

"And to make sure that it was to be the last time, you offered yourself to her."

"I couldn't help doing that."

"I don't say you could. I don't judge the facts at all. I leave them altogether to you; and you shall say what a man in my position ought to say to such a man as you have shown yourself."

"No, I will say." The door into the adjoining room was flung open, and Agatha flashed in from it.

Her father looked coldly at her impassioned face. "Have you been listening?" he asked.

"I have been hearing—"

- 99 -

"Oh!" As nearly as a man could, in bed, General Triscoe shrugged.

"I suppose I had, a right to be in my own room. I couldn't help hearing; and I was perfectly astonished at you, papa, the cruel way you went on, after all you've said about Mr. Stoller, and his getting no more than he deserved."

"That doesn't justify me," Burnamy began, but she cut him short almost as severely as she—had dealt with her father.

"Yes, it does! It justifies you perfectly! And his wanting you to falsify the whole thing afterwards, more than justifies you."

Neither of the men attempted anything in reply to her casuistry; they both looked equally posed by it, for different reasons; and Agatha went on as vehemently as before, addressing herself now to one and now to the other.

"And besides, if it didn't justify you, what you have done yourself would; and your never denying it, or trying to excuse it, makes it the same as if you hadn't done it, as far as you are concerned; and that is all I care for." Burnamy started, as if with the sense of having heard something like this before, and with surprise at hearing it now; and she flushed a little as she added tremulously, "And I should never, never blame you for it, after that; it's only trying to wriggle out of things which I despise, and you've never done that. And he simply had to come back," she turned to her father, "and tell me himself just how it was. And you said yourself, papa—or the same as said— that he had no right to suppose I was interested in his affairs unless he— unless—And I should never have forgiven him, if he hadn't told me then that he that he had come back because he—felt the way he did. I consider that that exonerated him for breaking his word, completely. If he hadn't broken his word I should have thought he had acted very cruelly and—and strangely. And ever since then, he has behaved so nobly, so honorably, so delicately, that I don't believe he would ever have said anything again—if I hadn't fairly forced him. Yes! Yes, I did!" she cried at a movement of remonstrance from Burnamy. "And I shall always be proud of you for it." Her father stared steadfastly at her, and he only lifted his eyebrows, for change of expression, when she went over to where Burnamy stood, and put her hand in his with a certain childlike impetuosity. "And as for the rest," she declared, "everything I have is his; just as everything of his would be mine if I had nothing. Or if he wishes to take me without anything, then he can have me so, and I sha'n't be afraid but we can get along somehow." She added, "I have managed without a maid, ever since I left home, and poverty has no terrors for me!"

LXVIII.

General Triscoe submitted to defeat with the patience which soldiers learn. He did not submit amiably; that would have been out of character, and perhaps out of reason; but Burnamy and Agatha were both so amiable that they supplied good-humor for all. They flaunted their rapture in her father's face as little as they could, but he may have found their serene satisfaction, their settled confidence in their fate, as hard to bear as a more boisterous happiness would have been.

It was agreed among them all that they were to return soon to America, and Burnamy was to find some sort of literary or journalistic employment in New York. She was much surer than he that this could be done with perfect ease; but they were of an equal mind that General Triscoe was not to be disturbed in any of his habits, or vexed in the tenor of his living; and until Burnamy was at least self-supporting there must be no talk of their being married.

The talk of their being engaged was quite enough for the time. It included complete and minute auto-biographies on both sides, reciprocal analyses of character, a scientifically exhaustive comparison of tastes, ideas and opinions; a profound study of their respective chins, noses, eyes, hands, heights, complexions, moles and freckles, with some account of their several friends.

In this occupation, which was profitably varied by the confession of what they had each thought and felt and dreamt concerning the other at every instant since they met, they passed rapidly the days which the persistent anxiety of General Triscoe interposed before the date of their leaving Weimar for Paris, where it was arranged that they should spend a month before sailing for New York. Burnamy had a notion, which Agatha approved, of trying for something there on the New York-Paris Chronicle; and if he got it they might not go home at once. His gains from that paper had eked out his copyright from his book, and had almost paid his expenses in getting the material which he had contributed to it. They were not so great, however, but that his gold reserve was reduced to less than a hundred dollars, counting the silver coinages which had remained to him in crossing and recrossing frontiers. He was at times dimly conscious of his finances, but he buoyantly disregarded the facts, as incompatible with his status as Agatha's betrothed, if not unworthy of his character as a lover in the abstract.

The afternoon before they were to leave Weimar, they spent mostly in the garden before the Grand-Ducal Museum, in a conference so important that when it came on to rain, at one moment, they put up Burnamy's umbrella, and continued to sit under it rather than interrupt the proceedings even to let Agatha go back to the hotel and look after her father's packing. Her own had been finished before dinner, so as to leave her the whole afternoon for their conference, and to allow her father to remain in undisturbed possession of his room as long as possible.

What chiefly remained to be put into the general's trunk were his coats and trousers, hanging in the closet, and August took these down, and carefully folded and packed them. Then, to make sure that nothing had been forgotten, Agatha put a chair into the closet when she came in, and stood on it to examine the shelf which stretched above the hooks.

There seemed at first to be nothing on it, and then there seemed to be something in the further corner, which when it was tiptoed for, proved to be a bouquet of flowers, not so faded as to seem very old; the blue satin ribbon which they were tied up with, and which hung down half a yard, was of entire freshness except far the dust of the shelf where it had lain.

Agatha backed out into the room with her find in her hand, and examined it near to, and then at arm's length. August stood by with a pair of the general's trousers lying across his outstretched hands, and as Agatha absently looked round at him, she caught a light of intelligence in his eyes which changed her whole psychological relation to the withered bouquet. Till then it had been a lifeless, meaningless bunch of flowers, which some one, for no motive, had tossed up on that dusty shelf in the closet. At August's smile it became something else. Still she asked lightly enough, "Was ist loss, August?"

His smile deepened and broadened. "Fur die Andere," he explained.

Agatha demanded in English, "What do you mean by feardy ondery?"

"Oddaw lehdy."

"Other lady?" August nodded, rejoicing in big success, and Agatha closed the door into her own room, where the general had been put for the time so as to be spared the annoyance of the packing; then she sat down with her hands in her lap, and the bouquet in her hands. "Now, August," she said very calmly, "I want you to tell me-ich wunsche Sie zu mir sagen—what other lady—wass andere Dame—these flowers belonged to—diese Blumen gehorte zu. Verstehen Sie?"

August nodded brightly, and with German carefully adjusted to Agatha's capacity, and with now and then a word or phrase of English, he conveyed that before she and her Herr Father had appeared, there had been in Weimar another American Fraulein with her Frau Mother; they had not indeed staid in that hotel, but had several times supped there with the young Herr Bornahmee, who was occupying that room before her Herr Father. The young Herr had been much about with these American Damen, driving and walking with them, and sometimes dining or supping with them at their hotel, The Elephant. August had sometimes carried notes to them from the young

Herr, and he had gone for the bouquet which the gracious Fraulein was holding, on the morning of the day that the American Damen left by the train for Hanover.

August was much helped and encouraged throughout by the friendly intelligence of the gracious Fraulein, who smiled radiantly in clearing up one dim point after another, and who now and then supplied the English analogues which he sought in his effort to render his German more luminous.

At the end she returned to the work of packing, in which she directed him, and sometimes assisted him with her own hands, having put the bouquet on the mantel to leave herself free. She took it up again and carried it into her own room, when she went with August to summon her father back to his. She bade August say to the young Herr, if he saw him, that she was going to sup with her father, and August gave her message to Burnamy, whom he met on the stairs coming down as he was going up with their tray.

Agatha usually supped with her father, but that evening Burnamy was less able than usual to bear her absence in the hotel dining-room, and he went up to a cafe in the town for his supper. He did not stay long, and when he returned his heart gave a joyful lift at sight of Agatha looking out from her balcony, as if she were looking for him. He made her a gay flourishing bow, lifting his hat high, and she came down to meet him at the hotel door. She had her hat on and jacket over one arm and she joined him at once for the farewell walk he proposed in what they had agreed to call their garden.

She moved a little ahead of him, and when they reached the place where they always sat, she shifted her jacket to the other arm and uncovered the hand in which she had been carrying the withered bouquet. "Here is something I found in your closet, when I was getting papa's things out."

"Why, what is it?" he asked innocently, as he took it from her.

"A bouquet, apparently," she answered, as he drew the long ribbons through his fingers, and looked at the flowers curiously, with his head aslant.

"Where did you get it?"

"On the shelf."

It seemed a long time before Burnamy said with a long sigh, as of final recollection, "Oh, yes," and then he said nothing; and they did not sit down, but stood looking at each other.

"Was it something you got for me, and forgot to give me?" she asked in a voice which would not have misled a woman, but which did its work with the young man.

He laughed and said, "Well, hardly! The general has been in the room ever since you came."

"Oh, yes. Then perhaps somebody left it there before you had the room?"

Burnamy was silent again, but at last he said, "No, I flung it up there I had forgotten all about it."

"And you wish me to forget about it, too?" Agatha asked in a gayety of tone that still deceived him.

"It would only be fair. You made me," he rejoined, and there was something so charming in his words and way, that she would have been glad to do it.

But she governed herself against the temptation and said, "Women are not good at forgetting, at least till they know what."

"Oh, I'll tell you, if you want to know," he said with a laugh, and at the words she—sank provisionally in their accustomed seat. He sat down beside her, but not so near as usual, and he waited so long before he began that it seemed as if he had forgotten again. "Why, it's nothing. Miss Etkins and her mother were here before you came, and this is a bouquet that I meant to give her at the train when she left. But I decided I wouldn't, and I threw it onto the shelf in the closet."

"May I ask why you thought of taking a bouquet to her at the train?"

"Well, she and her mother—I had been with them a good deal, and I thought it would be civil."

"And why did you decide not to be civil?"

"I didn't want it to look like more than civility."

"Were they here long?"

"About a week. They left just after the Marches came."

Agatha seemed not to heed the answer she had exacted. She sat reclined in the corner of the seat, with her head drooping. After an interval which was long to Burnamy she began to pull at a ring on the third finger of her left hand, absently, as if she did not know what she was doing; but when she had got it off she held it towards Burnamy and said quietly, "I think you had better have this again," and then she rose and moved slowly and weakly away.

He had taken the ring mechanically from her, and he stood a moment bewildered; then he pressed after her.

"Agatha, do you—you don't mean—"

"Yes," she said, without looking round at his face, which she knew was close to her shoulder. "It's over. It isn't what you've done. It's what you are. I believed in you, in spite of what you did to that man—and your coming back when you said you wouldn't—and—But I see now that what you did was you; it was your nature; and I can't believe in you any more."

"Agatha!" he implored. "You're not going to be so unjust! There was nothing between you and me when that girl was here! I had a right to—"

"Not if you really cared for me! Do you think I would have flirted with any one so soon, if I had cared for you as you pretended you did for me that night in Carlsbad? Oh, I don't say you're false. But you're fickle—"

"But I'm not fickle! From the first moment I saw you, I never cared for any one but you!"

"You have strange ways of showing your devotion. Well, say you are not fickle. Say, that I'm fickle. I am. I have changed my mind. I see that it would never do. I leave you free to follow all the turning and twisting of your fancy." She spoke rapidly, almost breathlessly, and she gave him no chance to get out the words that seemed to choke him. She began to run, but at the door of the hotel she stopped and waited till he came stupidly up. "I have a favor to ask, Mr. Burnamy. I beg you will not see me again, if you can help it before we go to-morrow. My father and I are indebted to you for too many kindnesses, and you mustn't take any more trouble on our account. August can see us off in the morning."

She nodded quickly, and was gone in-doors while he was yet struggling with his doubt of the reality of what had all so swiftly happened.

General Triscoe was still ignorant of any change in the status to which he had reconciled himself with so much difficulty, when he came down to get into the omnibus for the train. Till then he had been too proud to ask what had become of Burnamy, though he had wondered, but now he looked about and said impatiently, "I hope that young man isn't going to keep us waiting."

Agatha was pale and worn with sleeplessness, but she said firmly, "He isn't going, papa. I will tell you in the train. August will see to the tickets and the baggage."

August conspired with the traeger to get them a first-class compartment to themselves. But even with the advantages of this seclusion Agatha's confidences to her father were not full. She told her father that her engagement was broken for reasons that did not mean anything very wrong in Mr. Burnamy but that convinced her they could never be happy together. As she did not give the reasons, he found a natural difficulty in accepting them, and there was something in the situation which appealed strongly to his contrary-mindedness. Partly from this, partly from his sense of injury in being obliged so soon to adjust himself to new conditions, and partly from his comfortable feeling of security from an engagement to which his assent had been forced, he said, "I hope you're not making a mistake."

"Oh, no," she answered, and she attested her conviction by a burst of sobbing that lasted well on the way to the first stop of the train.

LXIX.

It would have been always twice as easy to go direct from Berlin to the Hague through Hanover; but the Marches decided to go by Frankfort and the Rhine, because they wished to revisit the famous river, which they remembered from their youth, and because they wished to stop at Dusseldorf, where Heinrich Heine was born. Without this Mrs. March, who kept her husband up to his early passion for the poet with a feeling that she was defending him from age in it, said that their silver wedding journey would not be complete; and he began himself to think that it would be interesting.

They took a sleeping-car for Frankfort and they woke early as people do in sleeping-cars everywhere. March dressed and went out for a cup of the same coffee of which sleeping-car buffets have the awful secret in Europe as well as America, and for a glimpse of the twilight landscape. One gray little town, towered and steepled and red-roofed within its mediaeval walls, looked as if it would have been warmer in something more. There was a heavy dew, if not a light frost, over all, and in places a pale fog began to lift from the low hills. Then the sun rose without dispersing the cold, which was afterwards so severe in their room at the Russischer Hof in Frankfort that in spite of the steam-radiators they sat shivering in all their wraps till breakfast-time.

There was no steam on in the radiators, of course; when they implored the portier for at least a lamp to warm their hands by he turned on all the electric lights without raising the temperature in the slightest degree. Amidst these modern comforts they were so miserable that they vowed each other to shun, as long as they were in Germany, or at least while the summer lasted, all hotels which were steam-heated and electric-lighted. They heated themselves somewhat with their wrath, and over their breakfast they relented so far as to suffer themselves a certain interest in the troops of all arms beginning to pass the hotel. They were fragments of the great parade, which had ended the day before, and they were now drifting back to their several quarters of the empire. Many of them were very picturesque, and they had for the boys and girls running before and beside them, the charm which armies and circus processions have for children everywhere. But their passage filled with cruel anxiety a large old dog whom his master had left harnessed to a milk-cart before the hotel door; from time to time he lifted up his voice, and called to the absentee with hoarse, deep barks that almost shook him from his feet.

The day continued blue and bright and cold, and the Marches gave the morning to a rapid survey of the city, glad that it was at least not wet. What afterwards chiefly remained to them was the impression of an old town as quaint almost and as Gothic as old Hamburg, and a new town, handsome and regular, and, in the sudden arrest of some streets, apparently overbuilt.

The modern architectural taste was of course Parisian; there is no other taste for the Germans; but in the prevailing absence of statues there was a relief from the most oppressive characteristic of the imperial capital which was a positive delight. Some sort of monument to the national victory over France there must have been; but it must have been unusually inoffensive, for it left no record of itself in the travellers' consciousness. They were aware of gardened squares and avenues, bordered by stately dwellings, of dignified civic edifices, and of a vast and splendid railroad station, such as the state builds even in minor European cities, but such as our paternal corporations have not yet given us anywhere in America. They went to the Zoological Garden, where they heard the customary Kalmucks at their public prayers behind a high board fence; and as pilgrims from the most plutrocratic country in the world March insisted that they must pay their devoirs at the shrine of the Rothschilds, whose natal banking-house they revered from the outside.

It was a pity, he said, that the Rothschilds were not on his letter of credit; he would have been willing to pay tribute to the Genius of Finance in the percentage on at least ten pounds. But he consoled himself by reflecting that he did not need the money; and he consoled Mrs. March for their failure to penetrate to the interior of the Rothschilds' birthplace by taking her to see the house where Goethe was born. The public is apparently much more expected there, and in the friendly place they were no doubt much more welcome than they would have been in the Rothschild house. Under that roof they renewed a happy moment of Weimar, which after the lapse of a week seemed already so remote. They wondered, as they mounted the stairs from the basement opening into a clean little court, how Burnamy was getting on, and whether it had yet come to that understanding between him and Agatha, which Mrs. March, at least, had meant to be inevitable. Then they became part of some such sight-seeing retinue as followed the custodian about in the Goethe horse in Weimar, and of an emotion indistinguishable from that of their fellow sight-seers. They could make sure, afterwards, of a personal pleasure in a certain prescient classicism of the house. It somehow recalled both the Goethe houses at Weimar, and it somehow recalled Italy. It is a separate house of two floors above the entrance, which opens to a little court or yard, and gives access by a decent stairway to the living-rooms. The chief of these is a sufficiently dignified parlor or salon, and the most important is the little chamber in the third story where the poet first opened his eyes to the light which he rejoiced in for so long a life, and which, dying, he implored to be with him more. It is as large as his death-chamber in Weimar, where he breathed this prayer, and it looks down into the Italian-looking court, where probably he noticed the world for the first time, and thought it a paved enclosure thirty or forty feet square. In the birth-room they keep his puppet theatre, and the place is fairly suggestive of his childhood; later, in his youth, he could look from the parlor windows and see the house where his earliest love dwelt. So much remains of Goethe in the place where he was born, and as such things go, it is not a little. The house is that of a prosperous and well-placed citizen, and speaks of the senatorial quality in his family which Heine says he was fond of recalling, rather than the sartorial quality of the ancestor who, again as Heine says, mended the Republic's breeches.

From the Goethe house, one drives by the Goethe monument to the Romer, the famous town-hall of the old free imperial city which Frankfort once was; and by this route the Marches drove to it, agreeing with their coachman that he was to keep as much in the sun as possible. It was still so cold that when they reached the Romer, and he stopped in a broad blaze of the only means of heating that they have in Frankfort in the summer, the travellers were loath to leave it for the chill interior, where the German emperors were elected for so many centuries. As soon as an emperor was chosen, in the great hall effigied round with the portraits of his predecessors, he hurried out in the balcony, ostensibly to show himself to the people, but really, March contended, to warm up a little in the sun. The balcony was undergoing repairs that day, and the travellers could not go out on it; but under the spell of the historic interest of the beautiful old Gothic place, they lingered in the interior till they were half-torpid with the cold. Then she abandoned to him the joint duty of viewing the cathedral, and hurried to their carriage where she basked in the sun till he came to her. He returned shivering, after a half-hour's absence, and pretended that she had missed the greatest thing in the world, but as he could never be got to say just what she had lost, and under the closest cross-examination could not prove that this cathedral was memorably different from hundreds of other fourteenth-century cathedrals, she remained in a lasting content with the easier part she had chosen. His only definite impression at the cathedral seemed to be confined to a Bostonian of gloomily correct type, whom he had seen doing it with his Baedeker, and not letting an object of interest escape; and his account of her fellow-townsman reconciled Mrs. March more and more to not having gone.

As it was warmer out-doors than in-doors at Frankfort, and as the breadth of sunshine increased with the approach of noon they gave the rest of the morning to driving about and ignorantly enjoying the outside of many Gothic churches, whose names even they did not trouble themselves to learn. They liked the river Main whenever they came to it, because it was so lately from Wurzburg, and because it was so beautiful with its bridges, old and new, and its boats of many patterns. They liked the market-place in front of the Romer not only because it was full of fascinating bargains in curious crockery and wooden-ware, but because there was scarcely any shade at all in it. They read from their Baedeker that until the end of the last century no Jew was suffered to enter the marketplace, and they rejoiced to find from all appearances that the Jews had been making up for their unjust exclusion ever since. They were almost as numerous there as the Anglo-Saxons were everywhere else in Frankfort. These, both of the English and American branches of the race, prevailed in the hotel diningroom, where the Marches had a mid-day dinner so good that it almost made amends for the steam-heating and electric-lighting.

As soon as possible after dinner they took the train for Mayence, and ran Rhinewards through a pretty country into what seemed a milder climate. It grew so much milder, apparently, that a lady in their compartment to whom March offered his forward-looking seat, ordered the window down when the guard came, without asking their leave. Then the climate proved much colder, and Mrs. March cowered under her shawls the rest of the way, and would not be entreated to look at the pleasant level landscape near, or the hills far off. He proposed to put up the window as peremptorily as it had been put down, but she stayed him with a hoarse whisper, "She may be another Baroness!" At first he did not know what she meant, then he remembered the lady whose claims to rank her presence had so poorly enforced on the way to Wurzburg, and he perceived that his wife was practising a wise forbearance with their fellow-passengers, and giving her a chance to turn out any sort of highhote she chose. She failed to profit by the opportunity; she remained simply a selfish, disagreeable woman, of no more perceptible distinction than their other fellow-passenger, a little commercial traveller from Vienna (they resolved from his appearance and the lettering on his valise that he was no other), who slept with a sort of passionate intensity all the way to Mayence.

LXX.

The Main widened and swam fuller as they approached the Rhine, and flooded the low-lying fields in-places with a pleasant effect under a wet sunset. When they reached the station in Mayence they drove interminably to the hotel they had chosen on the river-shore, through a city handsomer and cleaner than any American city they could think of, and great part of the way by a street of dwellings nobler, Mrs. March owned, than even Commonwealth Avenue in Boston. It was planted, like that, with double rows of trees, but lacked its green lawns; and at times the sign of Weinhandlung at a corner, betrayed that there was no such restriction against shops as keeps the Boston street so sacred. Otherwise they had to confess once more that any inferior city of Germany is of a more proper and dignified presence than the most parse-proud metropolis in America. To be sure, they said, the German towns had generally a thousand years' start; but all the same the fact galled them.

It was very bleak, though very beautiful when they stopped before their hotel on the Rhine, where all their impalpable memories of their visit to Mayence thirty years earlier precipitated themselves into something tangible. There were the reaches of the storied and fabled stream with its boats and bridges and wooded shores and islands; there were the spires and towers and roofs of the town on either bank crowding to the river's brink; and there within-doors was the stately portier in gold braid, and the smiling, bowing, hand-rubbing landlord, alluring them to his most expensive rooms, which so late in the season he would fain have had them take. But in a little elevator, that mounted slowly, very slowly, in the curve of the stairs, they went higher to something lower, and the landlord retired baked, and left them to the ministrations of the serving-men who arrived with their large and small baggage. All these retired in turn when they asked to have a fire lighted in the stove, without which Mrs. March would never have taken the fine stately rooms, and sent back a pretty young girl to do it. She came indignant, not because she had come lugging a heavy hod of coal and a great arm-load of wood, but because her sense of fitness was outraged by the strange demand.

"What!" she cried. "A fire in September!"

"Yes," March returned, inspired to miraculous aptness in his German by the exigency, "yes, if September is cold."

The girl looked at him, and then, either because she thought him mad, or liked him merry, burst into a loud laugh, and kindled the fire without a word more.

He lighted all the reluctant gas-jets in the vast gilt chandelier, and in less than half an hour the temperature of the place rose to at least sixty-five Fahrenheit, with every promise of going higher. Mrs. March made herself comfortable in a deep chair before the stove, and said she would have her supper there; and she bade him send her just such a supper of chicken and honey and tea as they had all had in Mayence when they supped in her aunt's parlor there all those years ago. He wished to compute the years, but she drove him out with an imploring cry, and he went down to a very gusty dining-room on the ground-floor, where he found himself alone with a young English couple and their little boy. They were friendly, intelligent people, and would have been conversable, apparently, but for the terrible cold of the husband, which he said he had contracted at the manoeuvres in Hombourg. March said he was going to Holland, and the Englishman was doubtful of the warmth which March expected to find there. He seemed to be suffering from a suspense of faith as to the warmth anywhere; from time to time the door of the dining-room self-opened in a silent, ghostly fashion into the court without, and let in a chilling draught about the legs of all, till the little English boy got down from his place and shut it.

He alone continued cheerful, for March's spirits certainly did not rise when some mumbling Americans came in and muttered over their meat at another table. He hated to own it, but he had to own that wherever he had met the two branches of the Anglo-Saxon race together in Europe, the elder had shown, by a superior chirpiness, to the disadvantage of the younger. The cast clothes of the old-fashioned British offishness seemed to have fallen to the American travellers who were trying to be correct and exemplary; and he would almost rather have had back the old-style bragging Americans whom he no longer saw. He asked of an agreeable fellow-countryman whom he found later in the reading-room, what had become of these; and this compatriot said he had travelled with one only the day before, who had posed before their whole compartment in his scorn of the German landscape, the German weather, the German government, the German railway management, and then turned out an American of German birth! March found his wife in great bodily comfort when he went back to her, but in trouble of mind about a clock which she had discovered standing on the lacquered iron top of the stove. It was a French clock, of architectural pretensions, in the taste of the first Empire, and it looked as if it had not been going since Napoleon occupied Mayence early in the century. But Mrs. March now had it sorely on her conscience where, in its danger from the heat of the stove, it rested with the weight of the Pantheon, whose classic form it recalled. She wondered that no one had noticed it before the fire was kindled, and she required her husband to remove it at once from the top of the stove to the mantel under the mirror, which was the natural habitat of such a clock. He said nothing could be simpler, but when he lifted it, it began to fall all apart, like a clock in the house of the Hoodoo. Its marble base dropped-off; its pillars tottered; its pediment swayed to one side. While Mrs. March lamented her hard fate, and implored him to hurry it together before any one came, he contrived to reconstruct it in its new place. Then they both breathed freer, and returned to sit down before the stove. But at the same moment they both saw, ineffaceably outlined on the lacquered top, the basal form of the clock. The chambermaid would see it in the morning; she would notice the removal of the clock, and would make a merit of reporting its ruin by the heat to the landlord, and in the end they would be mulcted of its value. Rather than suffer this wrong they agreed to restore it to its place, and, let it go to destruction upon its own terms. March painfully rebuilt it where he had found it, and they went to bed with a bad conscience to worse dreams.

He remembered, before he slept, the hour of his youth when he was in Mayence before, and was so care free that he had heard with impersonal joy two young American voices speaking English in the street under his window. One of them broke from the common talk with a gay burlesque of pathos in the line:

"Oh heavens! she cried, my Heeding country save!"

and then with a laughing good-night these unseen, unknown spirits of youth parted and departed. Who were they, and in what different places, with what cares or ills, had their joyous voices grown old, or fallen silent for evermore? It was a moonlight night, March remembered, and he remembered how he wished he were out in it with those merry fellows.

He nursed the memory and the wonder in his dreaming thought, and he woke early to other voices under his window. But now the voices, though young, were many and were German, and the march of feet and the stamp of hooves kept time with their singing. He drew his curtain and saw the street filled with broken squads of men, some afoot and some on horseback, some in uniform and some in civil dress with students' caps, loosely straggling on and roaring forth that song whose words he could not make out. At breakfast he asked the waiter what it all meant, and he said that these were conscripts whose service had expired with the late manoeuvres, and who were now going home. He promised March a translation of the song, but he never gave it; and perhaps the sense of their joyful home-going remained the more poetic with him because its utterance remained inarticulate.

March spent the rainy Sunday, on which they had fallen, in wandering about the little city alone. His wife said she was tired and would sit by the fire, and hear about Mayence when he came in. He went to the cathedral, which has its renown for beauty and antiquity, and he there added to his stock of useful information the fact that the people of Mayence seemed very Catholic and very devout. They proved it by preferring to any of the divine old Gothic shrines in the cathedral, an ugly baroque altar, which was everywhere hung about with votive offerings. A fashionably dressed young man and young girl sprinkled themselves with holy water as reverently as if they had been old and ragged. Some tourists strolled up and down the aisles with their red guide-books, and studied the objects of interest. A resplendent beadle in a cocked hat, and with along staff of authority posed before his own ecclesiastical consciousness in blue and silver. At the high altar a priest was saying mass, and March wondered whether his consciousness was as wholly ecclesiastical as the beadle's, or whether somewhere in it he felt the historical majesty, the long human consecration of the place.

He wandered at random in the town through streets German and quaint and old, and streets French and fine and new, and got back to the river, which he crossed on one of the several handsome bridges. The rough river looked chill under a sky of windy clouds, and he felt out of season, both as to the summer travel, and as to the journey he was making. The summer of life as well as the summer of that year was past. Better return to his own radiator in his flat on Stuyvesant Square; to the great ugly brutal town which, if it was not home to him, was as much home to him as to any one. A longing for New York welled up his heart, which was perhaps really a wish to be at work again. He said he must keep this from his wife, who seemed not very well, and whom he must try to cheer up when he returned to the hotel.

But they had not a very joyous afternoon, and the evening was no gayer. They said that if they had not ordered their letters sent to Dusseldorf they believed they should push on to Holland without stopping; and March would have liked to ask, Why not push on to America? But he forbore, and he was afterwards glad that he had done so.

In the morning their spirits rose with the sun, though the sun got up behind clouds as usual; and they were further animated by the imposition which the landlord practised upon them. After a distinct and repeated agreement as to the price of their rooms he charged them twice as much, and then made a merit of throwing off two marks out of the twenty he had plundered them of.

"Now I see," said Mrs. March, on their way down to the boat, "how fortunate it was that we baked his clock. You may laugh, but I believe we were the instruments of justice."

"Do you suppose that clock was never baked before?" asked her husband. "The landlord has his own arrangement with justice. When he overcharges his parting guests he says to his conscience, Well, they baked my clock."

LXXI.

The morning was raw, but it was something not to have it rainy; and the clouds that hung upon the hills and hid their tops were at least as fine as the long board signs advertising chocolate on the river banks. The smoke rising from the chimneys of the manufactories of Mayence was not so bad, either, when one got them in the distance a little; and March liked the way the river swam to the stems of the trees on the low grassy shores. It was like the Mississippi between St. Louis and Cairo in that, and it was yellow and thick, like the Mississippi, though he thought he remembered it blue and clear. A friendly German, of those who began to come aboard more and more at all the landings after leaving Mayence, assured him that he was right, and that the Rhine was unusually turbid from the unusual rains. March had his own belief that whatever the color of the Rhine might be the rains were not unusual, but he could not gainsay the friendly German.

Most of the passengers at starting were English and American; but they showed no prescience of the international affinition which has since realized itself, in their behavior toward one another. They held silently apart, and mingled only in the effect of one young man who kept the Marches in perpetual question whether he was a Bostonian or an Englishman. His look was Bostonian, but his accent was English; and was he a Bostonian who had been in England long enough to get the accent, or was he an Englishman who had been in Boston long enough to get the look? He wore a belated straw hat, and a thin sack-coat; and in the rush of the boat through the raw air they fancied him very cold, and longed to offer him one of their superabundant wraps. At times March actually lifted a shawl from his knees, feeling sure that the stranger was English and that he might make so bold with him; then at some glacial glint in the young man's eye, or at some petrific expression of his delicate face, he felt that he was a Bostonian, and lost courage and let the shawl sink again. March tried to forget him in the wonder of seeing the Germans begin to eat and drink, as soon as they came on boards either from the baskets they had brought with them, or from the boat's provision. But he prevailed, with his smile that was like a sneer, through all the events of the voyage; and took March's mind off the scenery with a sudden wrench when he came unexpectedly into view after a momentary disappearance. At the table d'hote, which was served when the landscape began to be less interesting, the guests were expected to hand their plates across the table to the stewards but to keep their knives and forks throughout the different courses, and at each of these partial changes March felt the young man's chilly eyes upon him, inculpating him for the semi-civilization of the management. At such times he knew that he was a Bostonian.

The weather cleared, as they descended the river, and under a sky at last cloudless, the Marches had moments of swift reversion to their former Rhine journey, when they were young and the purple light of love mantled the vineyarded hills along the shore, and flushed the castled steeps. The scene had lost nothing of the beauty they dimly remembered; there were certain features of it which seemed even fairer and grander than they remembered. The town of Bingen, where everybody who knows the poem was more or less born, was beautiful in spite of its factory chimneys, though there were no compensating castles near it; and the castles seemed as good as those of the theatre. Here and there some of them had been restored and were occupied, probably by robber barons who had gone into trade. Others were still ruinous, and there was now and then such a mere gray snag that March, at sight of it, involuntarily put his tongue to the broken tooth which he was keeping for the skill of the first American dentist.

For natural sublimity the Rhine scenery, as they recognized once more, does not compare with the Hudson scenery; and they recalled one point on the American river where the Central Road tunnels a jutting cliff, which might very well pass for the rock of the Loreley, where she dreams

'Solo sitting by the shores of old romance'

and the trains run in and out under her knees unheeded. "Still, still you know," March argued, "this is the Loreley on the Rhine, and not the Loreley on the Hudson; and I suppose that makes all the difference. Besides, the Rhine doesn't set up to be sublime; it only means to be storied and dreamy and romantic and it does it. And then we have really got no Mouse Tower; we might build one, to be sure."

"Well, we have got no denkmal, either," said his wife, meaning the national monument to the German reconquest of the Rhine, which they had just passed, "and that is something in our favor."

"It was too far off for us to see how ugly it was," he returned.

"The denkmal at Coblenz was so near that the bronze Emperor almost rode aboard the boat."

He could not answer such a piece of logic as that. He yielded, and began to praise the orcharded levels which now replaced the vine-purpled slopes of the upper river. He said they put him in mind of orchards that he had known in his boyhood; and they agreed that the supreme charm of travel, after all, was not in seeing something new and strange, but in finding something familiar and dear in the heart of the strangeness.

At Cologne they found this in the tumult of getting ashore with their baggage and driving from the steamboat landing to the railroad station, where they were to get their train for Dusseldorf an hour later. The station swarmed with travellers eating and drinking and smoking; but they escaped from it for a precious half of their golden hour, and gave the time to the great cathedral, which was built, a thousand years ago, just round the corner from the station, and is therefore very handy to it. Since they saw the cathedral last it had been finished, and now under a cloudless evening sky, it soared and swept upward like a pale flame. Within it was a bit over-clean, a bit bare, but without it was one of the great memories of the race, the record of a faith which wrought miracles of beauty, at least, if not piety.

The train gave the Marches another, and last, view of it as they slowly drew out of the city, and began to run through a level country walled with far-off hills; past fields of buckwheat showing their stems like coral under their black tops; past peasant houses changing their wonted shape to taller and narrower forms; past sluggish streams from which the mist rose and hung over the meadows, under a red sunset, glassy clear till the manifold factory chimneys of Dusseldorf stained it with their dun smoke.

This industrial greeting seemed odd from the town where Heinrich Heine was born; but when they had eaten their supper in the capital little hotel they found there, and went out for a stroll, they found nothing to remind them of the factories, and much to make them think of the poet. The moon, beautiful and perfect as a stage moon, came up over the shoulder of a church as they passed down a long street which they had all to themselves. Everybody seemed to have gone to bed, but at a certain corner a girl opened a window above them, and looked out at the moon.

When they returned to their hotel they found a highwalled garden facing it, full of black depths of foliage. In the night March woke and saw the moon standing over the garden, and silvering its leafy tops. This was really as it should be in the town where the idolized poet of his youth was born; the poet whom of all others he had adored, and who had once seemed like a living friend; who had been witness of his first love, and had helped him to speak it. His wife used to laugh at him for his Heine-worship in those days; but she had since come to share it, and she, even more than he, had insisted upon this pilgrimage. He thought long thoughts of the past, as he looked into the garden across the way, with an ache for his perished self and the dead companionship of his youth, all ghosts together in the silvered shadow. The trees shuddered in the night breeze, and its chill penetrated to him where he stood.

His wife called to him from her room, "What are you doing?"

"Oh, sentimentalizing," he answered boldly.

"Well, you will be sick," she said, and he crept back into bed again.

They had sat up late, talking in a glad excitement. But he woke early, as an elderly man is apt to do after broken slumbers, and left his wife still sleeping. He was not so eager for the poetic interests of the town as he had been the night before; he even deferred his curiosity for Heine's birth-house to the instructive conference which he had with his waiter at breakfast. After all, was not it more important to know something of the actual life of a simple common class of men than to indulge a faded fancy for the memory of a genius, which no amount of associations could feed again to its former bloom? The waiter said he was a Nuremberger, and had learned English in London where he had served a year for nothing. Afterwards, when he could speak three languages he got a pound a week, which seemed low for so many, though not so low as the one mark a day which he now received in Dusseldorf; in Berlin he paid the hotel two marks a day. March confided to him his secret trouble as to tips, and they tried vainly to enlighten each other as to what a just tip was.

He went to his banker's, and when he came back he found his wife with her breakfast eaten, and so eager for the exploration of Heine's birthplace that she heard with indifference of his failure to get any letters. It was too soon to expect them, she said, and then she showed him her plan, which she had been working out ever since she woke. It contained every place which Heine had mentioned, and she was determined not one should escape them. She examined him sharply upon his condition, accusing him of having taken cold when he got up in the night, and acquitting him with difficulty. She herself was perfectly well, but a little fagged, and they must have a carriage.

They set out in a lordly two-spanner, which took up half the little Bolkerstrasse where Heine was born, when they stopped across the way from his birthhouse, so that she might first take it all in from the outside before they entered it. It is a simple street, and not the cleanest of the streets in a town where most of them are rather dirty. Below the houses are shops, and the first story of Heine's house is a butcher shop, with sides of pork and mutton hanging in the windows; above, where the Heine family must once have lived, a gold-beater and a frame-maker displayed their signs.

But did the Heine family really once live there? The house looked so fresh and new that in spite of the tablet in its front affirming it the poet's birthplace, they doubted; and they were not reassured by the people who half halted as they passed, and stared at the strangers, so anomalously interested in the place. They dismounted, and crossed to the butcher shop where the provision man corroborated the tablet, but could not understand their wish to go up stairs. He did not try to prevent them, however, and they climbed to the first floor above, where a placard on the door declared it private and implored them not to knock. Was this the outcome of the inmate's despair from the intrusion of other pilgrims who had wised to see the Heine dwelling-rooms? They durst not knock and ask so much, and they sadly descended to the ground-floor, where they found a butcher boy of much greater apparent intelligence than the butcher himself, who told them that the building in front was as new as it looked, and the house where Heine was really born was the old house in the rear. He showed them this house, across a little court patched with mangy grass and lilac-bushes; and when they wished to visit it he led the way. The place was strewn both underfoot and overhead with feathers; it had once been all a garden out to the street, the boy said, but from these feathers, as well as the odor which prevailed, and the anxious behavior of a few hens left in the high coop at one side, it was plain that what remained of the garden was now a chicken slaughteryard. There was one well-grown tree, and the boy said it was of the poet's time; but when he let them into the house, he became vague as to the room where Heine was born; it was certain only that it was somewhere upstairs and that it could not be seen. The room where they stood was the frame-maker's shop, and they bought of him a small frame for a memorial. They bought of the butcher's boy, not so commercially, a branch of lilac; and they came away, thinking how much amused Heine himself would have been with their visit; how sadly, how merrily he would have mocked at their effort to revere his birthplace.

They were too old if not too wise to be daunted by their defeat, and they drove next to the old court garden beside the Rhine where the poet says he used to play with the little Veronika, and probably did not. At any rate, the garden is gone; the Schloss was burned down long ago; and nothing remains but a detached tower in which the good Elector Jan Wilhelm, of Heine's time, amused himself with his many mechanical inventions. The tower seemed to be in process of demolition, but an intelligent workman who came down out of it, was interested in the strangers' curiosity, and directed them to a place behind the Historical Museum where they could find a bit of the old garden. It consisted of two or three low trees, and under them the statue of the Elector by which Heine sat with the little Veronika, if he really did. A fresh gale blowing through the trees stirred the bushes that backed the statue, but not the laurel wreathing the Elector's head, and meeting in a neat point over his forehead. The laurel wreath is stone, like the rest of the Elector, who stands there smirking in marble ermine and armor, and resting his baton on the nose of a very small lion, who, in the exigencies of foreshortening, obligingly goes to nothing but a tail under the Elector's robe.

This was a prince who loved himself in effigy so much that he raised an equestrian statue to his own renown in the market-place, though he modestly refused the credit of it, and ascribed its erection to the affection of his subjects. You see him therein a full-bottomed wig, mounted on a rampant charger with a tail as big round as a barrel, and heavy enough to keep him from coming down on his fore legs as long as he likes to hold them up. It was to this horse's back that Heine clambered when a small boy, to see the French take formal possession of Dusseldorf; and he clung to the waist of the bronze Elector, who had just abdicated, while the burgomaster made a long speech, from the balcony of the Rathhaus, and the Electoral arms were taken down from its doorway.

The Rathhaus is a salad-dressing of German gothic and French rococo as to its architectural style, and is charming in its way, but the Marches were in the market-place for the sake of that moment of Heine's boyhood. They felt that he might have been the boy who stopped as he ran before them, and smacked the stomach of a large pumpkin lying at the feet of an old market-woman, and then dashed away before she could frame a protest against the indignity. From this incident they philosophized that the boys of Dusseldorf are as mischievous at the end of the century as they were at the beginning; and they felt the fascination that such a bounteous, unkempt old marketplace must have for the boys of any period. There were magnificent vegetables of all sorts in it, and if the fruits were meagre that was the fault of the rainy summer, perhaps. The market-place was very dirty, and so was the narrow street leading down from it to the Rhine, which ran swift as a mountain torrent along a slatternly quay. A bridge of boats crossing the stream shook in the rapid current, and a long procession of market carts passed slowly over, while a cluster of scows waited in picturesque patience for the draw to open.

They saw what a beautiful town that was for a boy to grow up in, and how many privileges it offered, how many dangers, how many chances for hairbreadth escapes. They chose that Heine must often have rushed shrieking joyfully down that foul alley to the Rhine with other boys; and they easily found a leaf-strewn stretch of the sluggish Dussel, in the Public Garden, where his playmate, the little Wilhelm, lost his life and saved the kitten's. They were not so sure of the avenue through which the poet saw the Emperor Napoleon come riding on his small white horse when he took possession of the Elector's dominions. But if it was that where the statue of the Kaiser Wilhelm I. comes riding on a horse led by two Victories, both poet and hero are avenged there on the accomplished fact. Defeated and humiliated France triumphs in the badness of that foolish denkmal (one of the worst in all denkmal-ridden Germany), and the memory of the singer whom the Hohenzollern family pride forbids honor in his native place, is immortal in its presence.

On the way back to their hotel, March made some reflections upon the open neglect, throughout Germany, of the greatest German lyrist, by which the poet might have profited if he had been present. He contended that it was not altogether an effect of Hohenzollern pride, which could not suffer a joke or two from the arch-humorist; but that Heine had said things of Germany herself which Germans might well have found unpardonable. He concluded that it would not do to be perfectly frank with one's own country. Though, to be sure, there would always be the question whether the Jew-born Heine had even a step-fatherland in the Germany he loved so tenderly and mocked so pitilessly. He had to own that if he were a negro poet he would not feel bound to measure terms in speaking of America, and he would not feel that his fame was in her keeping.

Upon the whole he blamed Heine less than Germany and he accused her of taking a shabby revenge, in trying to forget him; in the heat of his resentment that there should be no record of Heine in the city where he was born, March came near ignoring himself the fact that the poet Freiligrath was also born there. As for the famous Dusseldorf school of painting, which once filled the world with the worst art, he rejoiced that it was now so dead, and he grudged the glance which the beauty of the new Art Academy extorted from him. It is in the French taste, and is so far a monument to the continuance in one sort of that French supremacy, of which in another sort another denkmal celebrates the overthrow. Dusseldorf is not content with the denkmal of the Kaiser on horseback, with the two Victories for grooms; there is a second, which the Marches found when they strolled out again late in the afternoon. It is in the lovely park which lies in the heart of the city, and they felt in its presence the only emotion of sympathy which the many patriotic monuments of Germany awakened in them. It had dignity and repose, which these never had elsewhere; but it was perhaps not so much for the dying warrior and the pitying lion of the sculpture that their hearts were moved as for the gentle and mournful humanity of the inscription, which dropped into equivalent English verse in March's note-book:

Fame was enough for the Victors, and glory and verdurous laurel;
Tears by their mothers wept founded this image of stone.

To this they could forgive the vaunting record, on the reverse, of the German soldiers who died heroes in the war with France, the war with Austria, and even the war with poor little Denmark!

The morning had been bright and warm, and it was just that the afternoon should be dim and cold, with a pale sun looking through a September mist, which seemed to deepen the seclusion and silence of the forest reaches; for the park was really a forest of the German sort, as parks are apt to be in Germany. But it was beautiful, and they strayed through it, and sometimes sat down on the benches in its damp shadows, and said how much seemed to be done in Germany for the people's comfort and pleasure. In what was their own explicitly, as well as what was tacitly theirs, they were not so restricted as we were at home, and especially the children seemed made fondly and lovingly free of all public things. The Marches met troops of them in the forest, as they strolled slowly back by the winding Dussel to the gardened avenue leading to the park, and they found them everywhere gay and joyful. But their elders seemed subdued, and were silent. The strangers heard no sound of laughter in the streets of Dusseldorf, and they saw no smiling except on the part of a very old couple, whose meeting they witnessed and who grinned and cackled at each other like two children as they shook hands. Perhaps they were indeed children of that sad second childhood which one would rather not blossom back into.

In America, life is yet a joke with us, even when it is grotesque and shameful, as it so often is; for we think we can make it right when we choose. But there is no joking in Germany, between the first and second childhoods, unless behind closed doors. Even there, people do not joke above their breath about kings and emperors. If they joke about them in print, they take out their laugh in jail, for the press laws are severely enforced, and the prisons are full of able editors, serious as well as comic. Lese-majesty is a crime that searches sinners out in every walk of life, and it is said that in family jars a husband sometimes has the last word of his wife by accusing her of blaspheming the sovereign, and so having her silenced for three months at least behind penitential bars.

"Think," said March, "how simply I could adjust any differences of opinion between us in Dusseldorf."

"Don't!" his wife implored with a burst of feeling which surprised him. "I want to go home!"

They had been talking over their day, and planning their journey to Holland for the morrow, when it came to this outburst from her in the last half-hour before bed which they sat prolonging beside their stove.

"What! And not go to Holland? What is to become of my after-cure?"

"Oh, it's too late for that, now. We've used up the month running about, and tiring ourselves to death. I should like to rest a week—to get into my berth on the Norumbia and rest!"

"I guess the September gales would have something to say about that."

"I would risk the September gales."

LXXII.

In the morning March came home from his bankers gay with the day's provisional sunshine in his heart, and joyously expectant of his wife's pleasure in the letters he was bringing. There was one from each of their children, and there was one from Fulkerson, which March opened and read on the street, so as to intercept any unpleasant news there might be in them; there were two letters for Mrs. March which he knew without opening were from Miss Triscoe and Mrs. Adding respectively; Mrs. Adding's, from the postmarks, seemed to have been following them about for some time.

"They're all right at home," he said. "Do see what those people have been doing."

"I believe," she said, taking a knife from the breakfast tray beside her bed to cut the envelopes, "that you've really cared more about them all along than I have."

"No, I've only been anxious to be done with them."

She got the letters open, and holding one of them up in each hand she read them impartially and simultaneously; then she flung them both down, and turned her face into her pillow with an impulse of her inalienable girlishness. "Well, it is too silly."

March felt authorized to take them up and read them consecutively; when he had done, so he did not differ from his wife. In one case, Agatha had written to her dear Mrs. March that she and Burnamy had just that evening become engaged; Mrs. Adding, on her part owned a farther step, and announced her marriage to Mr. Kenby. Following immemorial usage in such matters Kenby had added a postscript affirming his happiness in unsparing terms, and in Agatha's letter there was an avowal of like effect from Burnamy. Agatha hinted her belief that her father would soon come to regard Burnamy as she did; and Mrs. Adding professed a certain humiliation in having realized that, after all her misgiving about him, Rose seemed rather relieved than otherwise, as if he were glad to have her off his hands.

"Well," said March, "with these troublesome affairs settled, I don't see what there is to keep us in Europe any longer, unless it's the consensus of opinion in Tom, Bella, and Fulkerson, that we ought to stay the winter."

"Stay the winter!" Mrs. March rose from her pillow, and clutched the home letters to her from the abeyance in which they had fallen on the coverlet while she was dealing with the others. "What do you mean?"

"It seems to have been prompted by a hint you let drop, which Tom has passed to Bella and Fulkerson."

"Oh, but that was before we left Carlsbad!" she protested, while she devoured the letters with her eyes, and continued to denounce the absurdity of the writers. Her son and daughter both urged that now their father and mother were over there, they had better stay as long as they enjoyed it, and that they certainly ought not to come home without going to Italy, where they had first met, and revisiting the places which they had seen together when they were young engaged people: without that their silver wedding journey would not be complete. Her son said that everything was going well with 'Every Other Week', and both himself and Mr. Fulkerson thought his father ought to spend the winter in Italy, and get a thorough rest. "Make a job of it, March," Fulkerson wrote, "and have a Sabbatical year while you're at it. You may not get another."

"Well, I can tell them," said Mrs. March indignantly, "we shall not do anything of the kind."

"Then you didn't mean it?"

"Mean it!" She stopped herself with a look at her husband, and asked gently, "Do you want to stay?"

"Well, I don't know," he answered vaguely. The fact was, he was sick of travel and of leisure; he was longing to be at home and at work again. But if there was to be any self-sacrifice which could be had, as it were, at a bargain; which could be fairly divided between them, and leave him the self and her the sacrifice, he was too experienced a husband not to see the advantage of it, or to refuse the merit. "I thought you wished to stay."

"Yes," she sighed, "I did. It has been very, very pleasant, and, if anything, I have over-enjoyed myself. We have gone romping through it like two young people, haven't we?"

"You have," he assented. "I have always felt the weight of my years in getting the baggage registered; they have made the baggage weigh more every time."

"And I've forgotten mine. Yes, I have. But the years haven't forgotten me, Basil, and now I remember them. I'm tired. It doesn't seem as if I could ever get up. But I dare say it's only a mood; it may be only a cold; and if you wish to stay, why—we will think it over."

"No, we won't, my dear," he said, with a generous shame for his hypocrisy if not with a pure generosity. "I've got all the good out of it that there was in it, for me, and I shouldn't go home any better six months hence than I should now. Italy will keep for another time, and so, for the matter of that, will Holland."

"No, no!" she interposed. "We won't give up Holland, whatever we do. I couldn't go home feeling that I had kept you out of your after-cure; and when we get there, no doubt the sea air will bring me up so that I shall want to go to Italy, too, again. Though it seems so far off, now! But go and see when the afternoon train for the Hague leaves, and I shall be ready. My mind's quite made up on that point."

"What a bundle of energy!" said her husband laughing down at her.

He went and asked about the train to the Hague, but only to satisfy a superficial conscience; for now he knew that they were both of one mind about going home. He also looked up the trains for London, and found that they could get there by way of Ostend in fourteen hours. Then he went back to the banker's, and with the help of the Paris-New York Chronicle which he found there, he got the sailings of the first steamers home. After that he strolled about the streets for a last impression of Dusseldorf, but it was rather blurred by the constantly recurring pull of his thoughts toward America, and he ended by turning abruptly at a certain corner, and going to his hotel.

He found his wife dressed, but fallen again on her bed, beside which her breakfast stood still untasted; her smile responded wanly to his brightness. "I'm not well, my dear," she said. "I don't believe I could get off to the Hague this afternoon."

"Could you to Liverpool?" he returned.

"To Liverpool?" she gasped. "What do you mean?"

"Merely that the Cupania is sailing on the twentieth, and I've telegraphed to know if we can get a room. I'm afraid it won't be a good one, but she's the first boat out, and—"

"No, indeed, we won't go to Liverpool, and we will never go home till you've had your after-cure in Holland." She was very firm in this, but she added, "We will stay another night, here, and go to the Hague tomorrow. Sit down, and let us talk it over. Where were we?"

She lay down on the sofa, and he put a shawl over her. "We were just starting for Liverpool."

"No, no we weren't! Don't say such things, dearest! I want you to help me sum it all, up. You think it's been a success, don't you?"

"As a cure?"

"No, as a silver wedding journey?"

"Perfectly howling."

"I do think we've had a good time. I never expected to enjoy myself so much again in the world. I didn't suppose I should ever take so much interest in anything. It shows that when we choose to get out of our rut we shall always find life as fresh and delightful as ever. There is nothing to prevent our coming any year, now that Tom's shown himself so capable, and having another silver wedding journey. I don't like to think of it's being confined to Germany quite."

"Oh, I don't know. We can always talk of it as our German-Silver Wedding Journey."

"That's true. But nobody would understand nowadays what you meant by German-silver; it's perfectly gone out. How ugly it was! A sort of greasy yellowish stuff, always getting worn through; I believe it was made worn through. Aunt Mary had a castor of it, that I can remember when I was a child; it went into the kitchen long before I grew up. Would a joke like that console you for the loss of Italy?"

"It would go far to do it. And as a German-Silver Wedding Journey, it's certainly been very complete."

"What do you mean?"

"It's given us a representative variety of German cities. First we had Hamburg, you know, a great modern commercial centre."

"Yes! Go on!"

"Then we had Leipsic, the academic."

"Yes!"

"Then Carlsbad, the supreme type of a German health resort; then Nuremberg, the mediaeval; then Anspach, the extinct princely capital; then Wurzburg, the ecclesiastical rococo; then Weimar, for the literature of a great epoch; then imperial Berlin; then Frankfort, the memory of the old free city; then Dusseldorf, the centre of the most poignant personal interest in the world—I don't see how we could have done better, if we'd planned it all, and not acted from successive impulses."

"It's been grand; it's been perfect! As German-Silver Wedding Journey it's perfect—it seems as if it had been ordered! But I will never let you give up Holland! No, we will go this afternoon, and when I get to Schevleningen, I'll go to bed, and stay there, till you've completed your after-cure."

"Do you think that will be wildly gay for the convalescent?"

She suddenly began to cry. "Oh, dearest, what shall we do? I feel perfectly broken down. I'm afraid I'm going to be sick—and away from home! How could you ever let me overdo, so?" She put her handkerchief to her eyes, and turned her face into the sofa pillow.

This was rather hard upon him, whom her vivid energy and inextinguishable interest had not permitted a moment's respite from pleasure since they left Carlsbad. But he had been married, too long not to understand that her blame of him was only a form of self-reproach for her own self-forgetfulness. She had not remembered that she was no longer young till she had come to what he saw was a nervous collapse. The fact had its pathos and its poetry which no one could have felt more keenly than he. If it also had its inconvenience and its danger he realized these too.

"Isabel," he said, "we are going home."

"Very well, then it will be your doing."

"Quite. Do you think you could stand it as far as Cologne? We get the sleeping-car there, and you can lie down the rest of the way to Ostend."

"This afternoon? Why I'm perfectly strong; it's merely my nerves that are gone." She sat up, and wiped her eyes. "But Basil! If you're doing this for me—"

"I'm doing it for myself," said March, as he went out of the room.

She stood the journey perfectly well, and in the passage to Dover she suffered so little from the rough weather that she was an example to many robust matrons who filled the ladies' cabin with the noise of their anguish during the night. She would have insisted upon taking the first train up to London, if March had not represented that this would not expedite the sailing of the Cupania, and that she might as well stay the forenoon at the convenient railway hotel, and rest. It was not quite his ideal of repose that the first people they saw in the coffee-room when they went to breakfast should be Kenby and Rose Adding, who were having their tea and toast and eggs together in the greatest apparent good-fellowship. He saw his wife shrink back involuntarily from the encounter, but this was only to gather force for it; and the next moment she was upon them in all the joy of the surprise. Then March allowed himself to be as glad as the others both seemed, and he shook hands with Kenby while his wife kissed Rose; and they all talked at once. In the confusion of tongues it was presently intelligible that Mrs. Kenby was going to be down in a few minutes; and Kenby took March into his confidence with a smile which was, almost a wink in explaining that he knew how it was with the ladies. He said that Rose and he usually got down to breakfast first, and when he had listened inattentively to Mrs. March's apology for being on her way home, he told her that she was lucky not to have gone to Schevleningen, where she and March would have frozen to death. He said that they were going to spend September at a little place on the English coast, near by, where he had been the day before with Rose to look at lodgings, and where you could bathe all through the month. He was not surprised that the Marches were going home, and said, Well, that was their original plan, wasn't it?

Mrs. Kenby, appearing upon this, pretended to know better, after the outburst of joyful greeting with the Marches; and intelligently reminded Kenby that he knew the Marches had intended to pass the winter in Paris. She was looking extremely pretty, but she wished only to make them see how well Rose was looking, and she put her arm round his shoulders as she spoke, Schevleningen had done wonders for him, but it was fearfully cold there, and now they were expecting everything from Westgate, where she advised March to come, too, for his after-cure: she recollected in time to say, She forgot they were on their way home. She added that she did not know when she should return; she was merely a passenger, now; she left everything to the men of the family. She had, in fact, the air of having thrown off every responsibility, but in supremacy, not submission. She was always ordering Kenby about; she sent him for her handkerchief, and her rings which she had left either in the tray of her trunk, or on the pin-cushion, or on the wash-stand or somewhere, and forbade him to come back without them. He asked for her keys, and then with a joyful scream she owned that she had left the door-key in the door and the whole bunch of trunk-keys in her trunk; and Kenby treated it all as the greatest joke; Rose, too, seemed to think that Kenby would make everything come right, and he had lost that look of anxiety which he used to have; at the most he showed a friendly sympathy for Kenby, for whose sake he seemed mortified at her. He was unable to regard his mother as the delightful joke which she appeared to Kenby, but that was merely temperamental; and he was never distressed except when she behaved with unreasonable caprice at Kenby's cost.

As for Kenby himself he betrayed no dissatisfaction with his fate to March. He perhaps no longer regarded his wife as that strong character which he had sometimes wearied March by celebrating; but she was still the most brilliant intelligence, and her charm seemed only to have grown with his perception of its wilful limitations. He did not want to talk about her so much; he wanted rather to talk about Rose, his health, his education, his nature, and what was best to do for him. The two were on terms of a confidence and affection which perpetually amused Mrs. Kenby, but which left the sympathetic witness nothing to desire in their relation.

They all came to the train when the Marches started up to London, and stood waving to them as they pulled out of the station. "Well, I can't see but that's all right," he said as he sank back in his seat with a sigh of relief. "I never supposed we should get out of their marriage half so well, and I don't feel that you quite made the match either, my dear."

She was forced to agree with him that the Kenbys seemed happy together, and that there was nothing to fear for Rose in their happiness. He would be as tenderly cared for by Kenby as he could have been by his mother, and far more judiciously. She owned that she had trembled for him till she had seen them all together; and now she should never tremble again.

"Well?" March prompted, at a certain inconclusiveness in her tone rather than her words.

"Well, you can see that it, isn't ideal."

"Why isn't it ideal? I suppose you think that the marriage of Burnamy and Agatha Triscoe will be ideal, with their ignorances and inexperiences and illusions."

"Yes! It's the illusions: no marriage can be perfect without them, and at their age the Kenbys can't have them."

"Kenby is a solid mass of illusion. And I believe that people can go and get as many new illusions as they want, whenever they've lost their old ones."

"Yes, but the new illusions won't wear so well; and in marriage you want illusions that will last. No; you needn't talk to me. It's all very well, but it isn't ideal."

March laughed. "Ideal! What is ideal?"

"Going home!" she said with such passion that he had not the heart to point out that they were merely returning to their old duties, cares and pains, with the worn-out illusion that these would be altogether different when they took them up again.

LXXIII.

In fulfilment of another ideal Mrs. March took straightway to her berth when she got on board the Cupania, and to her husband's admiration she remained there till the day before they reached New York. Her theory was that the complete rest would do more than anything else to calm her shaken nerves; and she did not admit into her calculations the chances of adverse weather which March would not suggest as probable in the last week in September. The event justified her unconscious faith. The ship's run was of unparalled swiftness, even for the Cupania, and of unparalled smoothness. For days the sea was as sleek as oil; the racks were never on the tables once; the voyage was of the sort which those who make it no more believe in at the time than those whom they afterwards weary in boasting of it.

The ship was very full, but Mrs. March did not show the slightest curiosity to know who her fellow-passengers were. She said that she wished to be let perfectly alone, even by her own emotions, and for this reason she forbade March to bring her a list of the passengers till after they had left Queenstown lest it should be too exciting. He did not take the trouble to look it up, therefore; and the first night out he saw no one whom he knew at dinner; but the next morning at breakfast he found himself to his great satisfaction at the same table with the Eltwins. They were so much at ease with him that even Mrs. Eltwin took part in the talk, and told him how they had spent the time of her husband's rigorous after-cure in Switzerland, and now he was going home much better than they had expected. She said they had rather thought of spending the winter in Europe, but had given it up because they were both a little homesick. March confessed that this was exactly the case with his wife and himself; and he had to add that Mrs. March was not very well otherwise, and he should be glad to be at home on her account. The recurrence of the word home seemed to deepen Eltwin's habitual gloom, and Mrs. Eltwin hastened to leave the subject of their return for inquiry into Mrs. March's condition; her interest did not so far overcome her shyness that she ventured to propose a visit to her; and March found that the fact of the Eltwins' presence on board did not agitate his wife. It seemed rather to comfort her, and she said she hoped he would see all he could of the poor old things. She asked if he had met any one else he knew, and he was able to tell her that there seemed to be a good many swells on board, and this cheered her very much, though he did not know them; she liked to be near the rose, though it was not a flower that she really cared for.

She did not ask who the swells were, and March took no trouble to find out. He took no trouble to get a passenger-list, and he had the more trouble when he tried at last; the lists seemed to have all vanished, as they have a habit of doing, after the first day; the one that he made interest for with the head steward was a second-hand copy, and had no one he knew in it but the Eltwins. The social solitude, however, was rather favorable to certain other impressions. There seemed even more elderly people than there were on the Norumbia; the human atmosphere was gray and sober; there was nothing of the gay expansion of the outward voyage; there was little talking or laughing among those autumnal men who were going seriously and anxiously home, with faces fiercely set for the coming grapple; or necks meekly bowed for the yoke. They had eaten their cake, and it had been good, but there remained a discomfort in the digestion. They sat about in silence, and March fancied that the flown summer was as dreamlike to each of them as it now was to him. He hated to be of their dreary company, but spiritually he knew that he was of it; and he vainly turned to cheer himself with the younger passengers. Some matrons who went about clad in furs amused him, for they must have been unpleasantly warm in their jackets and boas; nothing but the hope of being able to tell the customs inspector with a good conscience that the things had been worn, would have sustained one lady draped from head to foot in Astrakhan.

They were all getting themselves ready for the fray or the play of the coming winter; but there seemed nothing joyous in the preparation. There were many young girls, as there always are everywhere, but there were not many young men, and such as there were kept to the smoking-room. There was no sign of flirtation among them; he would have given much for a moment of the pivotal girl, to see whether she could have brightened those gloomy surfaces with her impartial lamp. March wished that he could have brought some report from the outer world to cheer his wife, as he descended to their state-room. They had taken what they could get at the eleventh hour, and they had got no such ideal room as they had in the Norumbia. It was, as Mrs. March graphically said, a basement room. It was on the north side of the ship, which is a cold exposure, and if there had been any sun it could not have got into their window, which was half the time under water. The green waves, laced with foam, hissed as they ran across the port; and the electric fan in the corridor moaned like the wind in a gable.

He felt a sinking of the heart as he pushed the state-room door open, and looked at his wife lying with her face turned to the wall; and he was going to withdraw, thinking her asleep, when she said quietly, "Are we going down?"

"Not that I know of," he answered with a gayety he did not feel. "But I'll ask the head steward."

She put out her hand behind her for him to take, and clutched his fingers convulsively. "If I'm never any better, you will always remember this happy, summer, won't you? Oh, it's been such a happy summer! It has been one long joy, one continued triumph! But it was too late; we were too old; and it's broken me."

The time had been when he would have attempted comfort; when he would have tried mocking; but that time was long past; he could only pray inwardly for some sort of diversion, but what it was to be in their barren circumstance he was obliged to leave altogether to Providence. He ventured, pending an answer to his prayers upon the question, "Don't you think I'd better see the doctor, and get you some sort of tonic?"

She suddenly turned and faced him. "The doctor! Why, I'm not sick, Basil! If you can see the purser and get our rooms changed, or do something to stop those waves from slapping against that horrible blinking one-eyed window, you can save my life; but no tonic is going to help me."

She turned her face from him again, and buried it in the bedclothes, while he looked desperately at the racing waves, and the port that seemed to open and shut like a weary eye.

"Oh, go away!" she implored. "I shall be better presently, but if you stand there like that—Go and see if you can't get some other room, where I needn't feel as if I were drowning, all the way over."

He obeyed, so far as to go away at once, and having once started, he did not stop short of the purser's office. He made an excuse of getting greenbacks for some English bank-notes, and then he said casually that he supposed there would be no chance of having his room on the lower deck changed for something a little less intimate with the sea. The purser was not there to take the humorous view, but he conceived that March wanted something higher up, and he was able to offer him a room of those on the promenade where he had seen swells going in and out, for six hundred dollars. March did not blench, but said he would get his wife to look at it with him, and then he went out somewhat dizzily to take counsel with himself how he should put the matter to her. She would be sure to ask what the price of the new room would be, and he debated whether to take it and tell her some kindly lie about it, or trust to the bracing effect of the sum named in helping restore the lost balance of her nerves. He was not so rich that he could throw six hundred dollars away, but there might be worse things; and he walked up and down thinking. All at once it flashed upon him that he had better see the doctor, anyway, and find out whether there were not some last hope in medicine before he took the desperate step before him. He turned in half his course, and ran into a lady who had just emerged from the door of the promenade laden with wraps, and who dropped them all and clutched him to save herself from falling.

"Why, Mr. March!" she shrieked.

"Miss Triscoe!" he returned, in the astonishment which he shared with her to the extent of letting the shawls he had knocked from her hold lie between them till she began to pick them up herself. Then he joined her and in the relief of their common occupation they contrived to possess each other of the reason of their presence on, the same boat. She had sorrowed over Mrs. March's sad state, and he had grieved to hear that her father was going home because he was not at all well, before they found the general stretched out in his steamer-chair, and waiting with a grim impatience for his daughter.

"But how is it you're not in the passenger-list?" he inquired of them both, and Miss Triscoe explained that they had taken their passage at the last moment, too late, she supposed, to get into the list. They were in London, and had run down to Liverpool on the chance of getting berths. Beyond this she was not definite, and there was an absence of Burnamy not only from her company but from her conversation which mystified March through all his selfish preoccupations with his wife. She was a girl who had her reserves, but for a girl who had so lately and rapturously written them of her engagement, there was a silence concerning her betrothed that had almost positive quality. With his longing to try Miss Triscoe upon Mrs. March's malady as a remedial agent, he had now the desire to try Mrs. March upon Miss Triscoe's mystery as a solvent. She stood talking to him, and refusing to sit down and be wrapped up in the chair next her father. She said that if he were going to ask Mrs. March to let her come to her, it would not be worth while to sit down; and he hurried below.

"Did you get it?" asked his wife, without looking round, but not so apathetically as before.

"Oh, yes. That's all right. But now, Isabel, there's something I've got to tell you. You'd find it out, and you'd better know it at once."

She turned her face, and asked sternly, "What is it?"

Then he said, with, an almost equal severity, "Miss Triscoe is on board. Miss Triscoe-and-her-father. She wishes to come down and see you."

Mrs. March sat up and began to twist her hair into shape. "And Burnamy?"

"There is no Burnamy physically, or so far as I can make out, spiritually. She didn't mention him, and I talked at least five minutes with her."

"Hand me my dressing-sack," said Mrs. March, "and poke those things on the sofa under the berth. Shut up that wash-stand, and pull the curtain across that hideous window. Stop! Throw those towels into your berth. Put my shoes, and your slippers into the shoe-bag on the door. Slip the brushes into that other bag. Beat the dent out of the sofa cushion that your head has made. Now!"

"Then—then you will see her?"

"See her!"

Her voice was so terrible that he fled before it, and he returned with Miss Triscoe in a dreamlike simultaneity. He remembered, as he led the way into his corridor, to apologize for bringing her down into a basement room.

"Oh, we're in the basement, too; it was all we could get," she said in words that ended within the state-room he opened to her. Then he went back and took her chair and wraps beside her father.

He let the general himself lead the way up to his health, which he was not slow in reaching, and was not quick in leaving. He reminded March of the state he had seen him in at Wurzburg, and he said it had gone from bad to worse with him. At Weimar he had taken to his bed and merely escaped from it with his life. Then they had tried Schevleningen for a week, where, he said in a tone of some injury, they had rather thought they might find them, the Marches. The air had been poison to him, and they had come over to England with some notion of Bournemouth; but the doctor in London had thought not, and urged their going home. "All Europe is damp, you know, and dark as a pocket in winter," he ended.

There had been nothing about Burnamy, and March decided that he must wait to see his wife if he wished to know anything, when the general, who had been silent, twisted his head towards him, and said without regard to the context, "It was complicated, at Weimar, by that young man in the most devilish way. Did my daughter write to Mrs. March about—Well it came to nothing, after all; and I don't understand how, to this day. I doubt if they do. It was some sort of quarrel, I suppose. I wasn't consulted in the matter either way. It appears that parents are not consulted in these trifling affairs, nowadays." He had married his daughter's mother in open defiance of her father; but in the glare of his daughter's wilfulness this fact had whitened into pious obedience. "I dare say I shall be told, by-and-by, and shall be expected to approve of the result."

A fancy possessed March that by operation of temperamental laws General Triscoe was no more satisfied with Burnamy's final rejection than with his acceptance. If the engagement was ever to be renewed, it might be another thing; but as it stood, March divined a certain favor for the young man in the general's attitude. But the affair was altogether too delicate for comment; the general's aristocratic frankness in dealing with it might have gone farther if his knowledge had been greater; but in any case March did not see how he could touch it. He could only say, He had always liked Burnamy, himself.

He had his good qualities, the general owned. He did not profess to understand the young men of our time; but certainly the fellow had the instincts of a gentleman. He had nothing to say against him, unless in that business with that man—what was his name?

"Stoller?" March prompted. "I don't excuse him in that, but I don't blame him so much, either. If punishment means atonement, he had the opportunity of making that right very suddenly, and if pardon means expunction, then I don't see why that offence hasn't been pretty well wiped out.

"Those things are not so simple as they used to seem," said the general, with a seriousness beyond his wont in things that did not immediately concern his own comfort or advantage.

LXXVI.

In the mean time Mrs. March and Miss Triscoe were discussing another offence of Burnamy's.

"It wasn't," said the girl, excitedly, after a plunge through all the minor facts to the heart of the matter, "that he hadn't a perfect right to do it, if he thought I didn't care for him. I had refused him at Carlsbad, and I had forbidden him to speak to me about—on the subject. But that was merely temporary, and he ought to have known it. He ought to have known that I couldn't accept him, on the spur of the moment, that way; and when he had come back, after going away in disgrace, before he had done anything to justify himself. I couldn't have kept my self-respect; and as it was I had the greatest difficulty; and he ought to have seen it. Of course he said afterwards that he didn't see it. But when—when I found out that SHE had been in Weimar, and all that time, while I had been suffering in Carlsbad and Wurzburg, and longing to see him—let him know how I was really feeling—he was flirting with that—that girl, then I saw that he was a false nature, and I determined to put an end to everything. And that is what I did; and I shall always think I—did right—and—"

The rest was lost in Agatha's handkerchief, which she put up to her eyes. Mrs. March watched her from her pillow keeping the girl's unoccupied hand in her own, and softly pressing it till the storm was past sufficiently to allow her to be heard.

Then she said, "Men are very strange—the best of them. And from the very fact that he was disappointed, he would be all the more apt to rush into a flirtation with somebody else."

Miss Triscoe took down her handkerchief from a face that had certainly not been beautified by grief. "I didn't blame him for the flirting; or not so much. It was his keeping it from me afterwards. He ought to have told me the very first instant we were engaged. But he didn't. He let it go on, and if I hadn't happened on that bouquet I might never have known anything about it. That is what I mean by—a false nature. I wouldn't have minded his deceiving me; but to let me deceive myself—Oh, it was too much!"

Agatha hid her face in her handkerchief again. She was perching on the edge of the berth, and Mrs. March said, with a glance, which she did not see, toward the sofa, "I'm afraid that's rather a hard seat for you.

"Oh, no, thank you! I'm perfectly comfortable—I like it—if you don't mind?"

Mrs. March pressed her hand for answer, and after another little delay, sighed and said, "They are not like us, and we cannot help it. They are more temporizing."

"How do you mean?" Agatha unmasked again.

"They can bear to keep things better than we can, and they trust to time to bring them right, or to come right of themselves."

"I don't think Mr. March would trust things to come right of themselves!" said Agatha in indignant accusal of Mrs. March's sincerity.

"Ah, that's just what he would do, my dear, and has done, all along; and I don't believe we could have lived through without it: we should have quarrelled ourselves into the grave!"

"Mrs. March!"

"Yes, indeed. I don't mean that he would ever deceive me. But he would let things go on, and hope that somehow they would come right without any fuss."

"Do you mean that he would let anybody deceive themselves?"

"I'm afraid he would—if he thought it would come right. It used to be a terrible trial to me; and it is yet, at times when I don't remember that he means nothing but good and kindness by it. Only the other day in Ansbach—how long ago it seems!—he let a poor old woman give him her son's address in Jersey City, and allowed her to believe he would look him up when we got back and tell him we had seen her. I don't believe, unless I keep right round after him, as we say in New England, that he'll ever go near the man."

Agatha looked daunted, but she said, "That is a very different thing."

"It isn't a different kind of thing. And it shows what men are,—the sweetest and best of them, that is. They are terribly apt to be—easy-going."

"Then you think I was all wrong?" the girl asked in a tremor.

"No, indeed! You were right, because you really expected perfection of him. You expected the ideal. And that's what makes all the trouble, in married life: we expect too much of each other—we each expect more of the other than we are willing to give or can give. If I had to begin over again, I should not expect anything at all, and then I should be sure of being radiantly happy. But all this talking and all this writing about love seems to turn our brains; we know that men are not perfect, even at our craziest, because women are not, but we expect perfection of them; and they seem to expect it of us, poor things! If we could keep on after we are in love just as we were before we were in love, and take nice things as favors and surprises, as we did in the beginning! But we get more and more greedy and exacting—"

"Do you think I was too exacting in wanting him to tell me everything after we were engaged?"

"No, I don't say that. But suppose he had put it off till you were married?" Agatha blushed a little, but not painfully, "Would it have been so bad? Then you might have thought that his flirting up to the last moment in his desperation was a very good joke. You would have understood better just how it was, and it might even have made you fonder of him. You might have seen that he had flirted with some one else because he was so heart-broken about you."

"Then you believe that if I could have waited till—till—but when I had found out, don't you see I couldn't wait? It would have been all very well if I hadn't known it till then. But as I did know it. Don't you see?"

"Yes, that certainly complicated it," Mrs. March admitted. "But I don't think, if he'd been a false nature, he'd have owned up as he did. You see, he didn't try to deny it; and that's a great point gained."

"Yes, that is true," said Agatha, with conviction. "I saw that afterwards. But you don't think, Mrs. March, that I was unjust or—or hasty?"

"No, indeed! You couldn't have done differently under the circumstances. You may be sure he felt that—he is so unselfish and generous—" Agatha began to weep into her handkerchief again; Mrs. March caressed her hand. "And it will certainly come right if you feel as you do."

"No," the girl protested. "He can never forgive me; it's all over, everything is over. It would make very little difference to me, what happened now—if the steamer broke her shaft, or anything. But if I can only believe I wasn't unjust—"

Mrs. March assured her once more that she had behaved with absolute impartiality; and she proved to her by a process of reasoning quite irrefragable that it was only a question of time, with which place had nothing to do, when she and Burnamy should come together again, and all should be made right between them. The fact that she did not know where he was, any more than Mrs. March herself, had nothing to do with the result; that was a mere detail, which would settle itself. She clinched her argument by confessing that her own engagement had been broken off, and that it had simply renewed itself. All you had to do was to keep willing it, and waiting. There was something very mysterious in it.

"And how long was it till—" Agatha faltered.

"Well, in our ease it was two years."

"Oh!" said the girl, but Mrs. March hastened to reassure her.

"But our case was very peculiar. I could see afterwards that it needn't have been two months, if I had been willing to acknowledge at once that I was in the wrong. I waited till we met."

"If I felt that I was in the wrong, I should write," said Agatha. "I shouldn't care what he thought of my doing it."

"Yes, the great thing is to make sure that you were wrong."

They remained talking so long, that March and the general had exhausted all the topics of common interest, and had even gone through those they did not care for. At last the general said, "I'm afraid my daughter will tire Mrs. March."

"Oh, I don't think she'll tire my wife. But do you want her?"

"Well, when you're going down."

"I think I'll take a turn about the deck, and start my circulation," said March, and he did so before he went below.

He found his wife up and dressed, and waiting provisionally on the sofa. "I thought I might as well go to lunch," she said, and then she told him about Agatha and Burnamy, and the means she had employed to comfort and encourage the girl. "And now, dearest, I want you to find out where Burnamy is, and give him a hint. You will, won't you! If you could have seen how unhappy she was!"

"I don't think I should have cared, and I'm certainly not going to meddle. I think Burnamy has got no more than he deserved, and that he's well rid of her. I can't imagine a broken engagement that would more completely meet my approval. As the case stands, they have my blessing."

"Don't say that, dearest! You know you don't mean it."

"I do; and I advise you to keep your hands off. You've done all and more than you ought to propitiate Miss Triscoe. You've offered yourself up, and you've offered me up—"

"No, no, Basil! I merely used you as an illustration of what men were—the best of them."

"And I can't observe," he continued, "that any one else has been considered in the matter. Is Miss Triscoe the sole sufferer by Burnamy's flirtation? What is the matter with a little compassion for the pivotal girl?"

"Now, you know you're not serious," said his wife; and though he would not admit this, he could not be seriously sorry for the new interest which she took in the affair. There was no longer any question of changing their state-room. Under the tonic influence of the excitement she did not go back to her berth after lunch, and she was up later after dinner than he could have advised. She was absorbed in Agatha, but in her liberation from her hypochondria, she began also to make a comparative study of the American swells, in the light of her late experience with the German highhotes. It is true that none of the swells gave her the opportunity of examining them at close range, as the highhotes had done. They kept to their, state-rooms mostly, where, after he thought she could bear it, March told her how near he had come to making her their equal by an outlay of six hundred dollars. She now shuddered at the thought; but she contended that in their magnificent exclusiveness they could give points to European princes; and that this showed again how when Americans did try to do a thing, they beat the world. Agatha Triscoe knew who they were, but she did not know them; they belonged to another kind of set; she spoke of them as "rich people," and she seemed content to keep away from them with Mrs. March and with the shy, silent old wife of Major Eltwin, to whom March sometimes found her talking.

He never found her father talking with Major Eltwin. General Triscoe had his own friends in the smoking-room, where he held forth in a certain corner on the chances of the approaching election in New York, and mocked their incredulity when he prophesied the success of Tammany and the return of the King. March himself much preferred Major Eltwin to the general and his friends; he lived back in the talk of the Ohioan into his own younger years in Indiana, and he was amused and touched to find how much the mid-Western life seemed still the same as he had known. The conditions had changed, but not so much as they had changed in the East and the farther West. The picture that the major drew of them in his own region was alluring; it made March homesick; though he knew that he should never go back to his native section. There was the comfort of kind in the major; and he had a vein of philosophy, spare but sweet, which March liked; he liked also the meekness which had come through sorrow upon a spirit which had once been proud.

They had both the elderly man's habit of early rising, and they usually found themselves together waiting impatiently for the cup of coffee, ingenuously bad, which they served on the Cupania not earlier than half past six, in strict observance of a rule of the line discouraging to people of their habits. March admired the vileness of the decoction, which he said could not be got anywhere out of the British Empire, and he asked Eltwin the first morning if he had noticed how instantly on the Channel boat they had dropped to it and to the sour, heavy, sodden British bread, from the spirited and airy Continental tradition of coffee and rolls.

The major confessed that he was no great hand to notice such things, and he said he supposed that if the line had never lost a passenger, and got you to New York in six days it had a right to feed you as it pleased; he surmised that if they could get their airing outside before they took their coffee, it would give the coffee a chance to taste better; and this was what they afterwards did. They met, well buttoned and well mined up, on the promenade when it was yet so early that they were not at once sure of each other in the twilight, and watched the morning planets pale east and west before the sun rose. Sometimes there were no paling planets and no rising sun, and a black sea, ridged with white, tossed under a low dark sky with dim rifts.

One morning, they saw the sun rise with a serenity and majesty which it rarely has outside of the theatre. The dawn began over that sea which was like the rumpled canvas imitations of the sea on the stage, under long mauve clouds bathed in solemn light. Above these, in the pale tender sky, two silver stars hung, and the steamer's smoke drifted across them like a thin dusky veil. To the right a bank of dun cloud began to burn crimson, and to burn brighter till it was like a low hill-side full of gorgeous rugosities fleeced with a dense dwarfish growth of autumnal shrubs. The whole eastern heaven softened and flushed through diaphanous mists; the west remained a livid mystery. The eastern masses and flakes of cloud began to kindle keenly; but the stars shone clearly, and then one star, till the tawny pink hid it. All the zenith reddened, but still the sun did not show except in the color of the brilliant clouds. At last the lurid horizon began to burn like a flame-shot smoke, and a fiercely bright disc edge pierced its level, and swiftly defined itself as the sun's orb.

Many thoughts went through March's mind; some of them were sad, but in some there was a touch of hopefulness. It might have been that beauty which consoled him for his years; somehow he felt himself, if no longer young, a part of the young immortal frame of things. His state was indefinable, but he longed to hint at it to his companion.

"Yes," said Eltwin, with a long deep sigh. "I feel as if I could walk out through that brightness and find her. I reckon that such hopes wouldn't be allowed to lie to us; that so many ages of men couldn't have fooled themselves so. I'm glad I've seen this." He was silent and they both remained watching the rising sun till they could not bear its splendor. "Now," said the major, "it must be time for that mud, as you call it." Over their coffee and crackers at the end of the table which they had to themselves, he resumed. "I was thinking all the time—we seem to think half a dozen things at once, and this was one of them—about a piece of business I've got to settle when I reach home; and perhaps you can advise me about it; you're an editor. I've got a newspaper on my hands; I reckon it would be a pretty good thing, if it had a chance; but I don't know what to do with it: I got it in trade with a fellow who has to go West for his lungs, but he's staying till I get back. What's become of that young chap—what's his name?—that went out with us?"

"Burnamy?" prompted March, rather breathlessly.

"Yes. Couldn't he take hold of it? I rather liked him. He's smart, isn't he?"

"Very," said March. "But I don't know where he is. I don't know that he would go into the country—. But he might, if—"

They entered provisionally into the case, and for argument's sake supposed that Burnamy would take hold of the major's paper if he could be got at. It really looked to March like a good chance for him, on Eltwin's showing; but he was not confident of Burnamy's turning up very soon, and he gave the major a pretty clear notion why, by entering into the young fellow's history for the last three months.

"Isn't it the very irony of fate?" he said to his wife when he found her in their room with a cup of the same mud he had been drinking, and reported the facts to her.

"Irony?" she said, with all the excitement he could have imagined or desired. "Nothing of the kind. It's a leading, if ever there was one. It will be the easiest thing in the world to find Burnamy. And out there she can sit on her steps!"

He slowly groped his way to her meaning, through the hypothesis of Burnamy's reconciliation and marriage with Agatha Triscoe, and their settlement in Major Eltwin's town under social conditions that implied a habit of spending the summer evenings on their front porch. While he was doing this she showered him with questions and conjectures and requisitions in which nothing but the impossibility of going ashore saved him from the instant devotion of all his energies to a world-wide, inquiry into Burnamy's whereabouts.

The next morning he was up before Major Eltwin got out, and found the second-cabin passengers free of the first-cabin promenade at an hour when their superiors were not using it. As he watched these inferiors, decent-looking, well-clad men and women, enjoying their privilege with a furtive air, and with stolen glances at him, he asked himself in what sort he was their superior, till the inquiry grew painful. Then he rose from his chair, and made his way to the place where the material barrier between them was lifted, and interested himself in a few of them who seemed too proud to avail themselves of his society on the terms made. A figure seized his attention with a sudden fascination of conjecture and rejection: the figure of a tall young man who came out on the promenade and without looking round, walked swiftly away to the bow of the ship, and stood there, looking down at the water in an attitude which was bewilderingly familiar. His movement, his posture, his dress, even, was that of Burnamy, and March, after a first flush of pleasure, felt a sickening repulsion in the notion of his presence. It would have been such a cheap performance on the part of life, which has all sorts of chances at command, and need not descend to the poor tricks of second-rate fiction; and he accused Burnamy of a complicity in the bad taste of the affair, though he realized, when he reflected, that if it were really Burnamy he must have sailed in as much unconsciousness of the Triscoes as he himself had done. He had probably got out of money and had hurried home while he had still enough to pay the second-cabin fare on the first boat back. Clearly he was not to blame, but life was to blame for such a shabby device; and March felt this so keenly that he wished to turn from the situation, and have nothing to do with it. He kept moving toward him, drawn by the fatal attraction, and at a few paces' distance the young man whirled about and showed him the face of a stranger.

March made some witless remark on the rapid course of the ship as it cut its way through the water of the bow; the stranger answered with a strong Lancashire accent; and in the talk which followed, he said he was going out to see the cotton-mills at Fall River and New Bedford, and he seemed hopeful of some advice or information from March; then he said he must go and try to get his Missus out; March understood him to mean his wife, and he hurried down to his own, to whom he related his hair-breadth escape from Burnamy.

"I don't call it an escape at all!" she declared. "I call it the greatest possible misfortune. If it had been Burnamy we could have brought them together at once, just when she has seen so clearly that she was in the wrong, and is feeling all broken up. There wouldn't have been any difficulty about his being in the second-cabin. We could have contrived to have them meet somehow. If the worst came to the worst you could have lent him money to pay the difference, and got him into the first-cabin."

"I could have taken that six-hundred-dollar room for him," said March, "and then he could have eaten with the swells."

She answered that now he was teasing; that he was fundamentally incapable of taking anything seriously; and in the end he retired before the stewardess bringing her first coffee, with a well-merited feeling that if it had not been for his triviality the young Lancashireman would really have been Burnamy.

LXXV.

Except for the first day and night out from Queenstown, when the ship rolled and pitched with straining and squeaking noises, and a thumping of the lifted screws, there was no rough weather, and at last the ocean was livid and oily, with a long swell, on which she swayed with no perceptible motion save from her machinery.

Most of the seamanship seemed to be done after dark, or in those early hours when March found the stewards cleaning the stairs, and the sailors scouring the promenades. He made little acquaintance with his fellow-passengers. One morning he almost spoke with an old Quaker lady whom he joined in looking at the Niagara flood which poured from the churning screws; but he did not quite get the words out. On the contrary he talked freely with an American who, bred horses on a farm near Boulogne, and was going home to the Horse Show; he had been thirty-five years out of the country, but he had preserved his Yankee accent in all its purity, and was the most typical-looking American on board. Now and then March walked up and down with a blond Mexican whom he found of the usual well-ordered Latin intelligence, but rather flavorless; at times he sat beside a nice Jew, who talked agreeably, but only about business; and he philosophized the race as so tiresome often because it seemed so often without philosophy. He made desperate attempts at times to interest himself in the pool-selling in the smoking-room where the betting on the ship's wonderful run was continual.

He thought that people talked less and less as they drew nearer home; but on the last day out there was a sudden expansion, and some whom he had not spoken with voluntarily addressed him. The sweet, soft air was like midsummer the water rippled gently, without a swell, blue under the clear sky, and the ship left a wide track that was silver in the sun. There were more sail; the first and second class baggage was got up and piled along the steerage deck.

Some people dressed a little more than usual for the last dinner which was earlier than usual, so as to be out of the way against the arrival which had been variously predicted at from five to seven-thirty. An indescribable nervousness culminated with the appearance of the customs officers on board, who spread their papers on cleared spaces of the dining-tables, and summoned the passengers to declare that they had nothing to declare, as a preliminary to being searched like thieves at the dock.

This ceremony proceeded while the Cupania made her way up the Narrows, and into the North River, where the flare of lights from the crazy steeps and cliffs of architecture on the New York shore seemed a persistence of the last Fourth of July pyrotechnics. March blushed for the grotesque splendor of the spectacle, and was confounded to find some Englishmen admiring it, till he remembered that aesthetics were not the strong point of our race. His wife sat hand in hand with Miss Triscoe, and from time to time made him count the pieces of small baggage in the keeping of their steward; while General Triscoe held aloof in a sarcastic calm.

The steamer groped into her dock; the gangways were lifted to her side; the passengers fumbled and stumbled down their incline, and at the bottom the Marches found themselves respectively in the arms of their son and daughter. They all began talking at once, and ignoring and trying to remember the Triscoes to whom the young Marches were presented. Bella did her best to be polite to Agatha, and Tom offered to get an inspector for the general at the same time as for his father. Then March, remorsefully remembered the Eltwins, and looked about for them, so that his son might get them an inspector too. He found the major already in the hands of an inspector, who was passing all his pieces after carelessly looking into one: the official who received the declarations on board had noted a Grand Army button like his own in the major's lapel, and had marked his fellow-veteran's paper with the mystic sign which procures for the bearer the honor of being promptly treated as a smuggler, while the less favored have to wait longer for this indignity at the hands of their government. When March's own inspector came he was as civil and lenient as our hateful law allows; when he had finished March tried to put a bank-note in his hand, and was brought to a just shame by his refusal of it. The bed-room steward keeping guard over the baggage helped put-it together after the search, and protested that March had feed him so handsomely that he would stay there with it as long as they wished. This partly restored March's self-respect, and he could share in General Triscoe's indignation with the Treasury ruling which obliged him to pay duty on his own purchases in excess of the hundred-dollar limit, though his daughter had brought nothing, and they jointly came far within the limit for two.

He found that the Triscoes were going to a quiet old hotel on the way to Stuyvesant Square, quite in his own neighborhood, and he quickly arranged for all the ladies and the general to drive together while he was to follow with his son on foot and by car. They got away from the scene of the customs' havoc while the steamer shed, with its vast darkness dimly lit by its many lamps, still showed like a battle-field where the inspectors groped among the scattered baggage like details from the victorious army searching for the wounded. His son clapped him on the shoulder when he suggested this notion, and said he was the same old father; and they got home as gayly together as the dispiriting influences of the New York ugliness would permit. It was still in those good and decent times, now so remote, when the city got something for the money paid out to keep its streets clean, and those they passed through were not foul but merely mean.

The ignoble effect culminated when they came into Broadway, and found its sidewalks, at an hour when those of any European metropolis would have been brilliant with life, as unpeopled as those of a minor country town, while long processions of cable-cars carted heaps of men and women up and down the thoroughfare amidst the deformities of the architecture.

The next morning the March family breakfasted late after an evening prolonged beyond midnight in spite of half-hourly agreements that now they must really all go to bed. The children had both to recognize again and again how well their parents were looking; Tom had to tell his father about the condition of 'Every Other Week'; Bella had to explain to her mother how sorry her husband was that he could not come on to meet them with her, but was coming a week later to take her home, and then she would know the reason why they could not all, go back to Chicago with him: it was just the place for her father to live, for everybody to live. At breakfast she renewed the reasoning with which she had maintained her position the night before; the travellers entered into a full expression of their joy at being home again; March asked what had become of that stray parrot which they had left in the tree-top the morning they started; and Mrs. March declared that this was the last Silver Wedding Journey she ever wished to take, and tried to convince them all that she had been on the verge of nervous collapse when she reached the ship. They sat at table till she discovered that it was very nearly eleven o'clock, and said it was disgraceful.

Before they rose, there was a ring at the door, and a card was brought in to Tom. He glanced at it, and said to his father, "Oh, yes! This man has been haunting the office for the last three days. He's got to leave to-day, and as it seemed to be rather a case of life and death with him, I said he'd probably find you here this morning. But if you don't want to see him, I can put him off till afternoon, I suppose."

He tossed the card to his father, who looked at it quietly, and then gave it to his wife. "Perhaps I'd as well see him?"

"See him!" she returned in accents in which all the intensity of her soul was centred. By an effort of self-control which no words can convey a just sense of she remained with her children, while her husband with a laugh more teasing than can be imagined went into the drawing-room to meet Burnamy.

The poor fellow was in an effect of belated summer as to clothes, and he looked not merely haggard but shabby. He made an effort for dignity as well as gayety, however, in stating himself to March, with many apologies for his persistency. But, he said, he was on his way West, and he was anxious to know whether there was any chance of his 'Kasper Hauler' paper being taken if he finished it up. March would have been a far harder-hearted editor than he was, if he could have discouraged the suppliant before him. He said he would take the Kasper Hauler paper and add a band of music to the usual rate of ten dollars a thousand words. Then Burnamy's dignity gave way, if not his gayety; he began to laugh, and suddenly he broke down and confessed that he had come home in the steerage; and was at his last cent, beyond his fare to Chicago. His straw hat looked like a withered leaf in the light of his sad facts; his thin overcoat affected March's imagination as something like the diaphanous cast shell of a locust, hopelessly resumed for comfort at the approach of autumn. He made Burnamy sit down, after he had once risen, and he told him of Major Eltwin's wish to see him; and he promised to go round with him to the major's hotel before the Eltwins left town that afternoon.

While he prolonged the interview in this way, Mrs. March was kept from breaking in upon them only by the psychical experiment which she was making with the help and sympathy of her daughter at the window of the dining-room which looked up Sixteenth Street. At the first hint she gave of the emotional situation which Burnamy was a main part of, her son; with the brutal contempt of young men for other young men's love affairs, said he must go to the office; he bade his mother tell his father there was no need of his coming down that day, and he left the two women together. This gave the mother a chance to develop the whole fact to the daughter with telegrammic rapidity and brevity, and then to enrich the first-outline with innumerable details, while they both remained at the window, and Mrs. March said at two-minutely intervals, with no sense of iteration for either of them, "I told her to come in the morning, if she felt like it, and I know she will. But if she doesn't, I shall say there is nothing in fate, or Providence either. At any rate I'm going to stay here and keep longing for her, and we'll see whether there's anything in that silly theory of your father's. I don't believe there is," she said, to be on the safe side.

Even when she saw Agatha Triscoe enter the park gate on Rutherford Place, she saved herself from disappointment by declaring that she was not coming across to their house. As the girl persisted in coming and coming, and at last came so near that she caught sight of Mrs. March at the window and nodded, the mother turned ungratefully upon her daughter, and drove her away to her own room, so that no society detail should hinder the divine chance. She went to the door herself when Agatha rang, and then she was going to open the way into the parlor where March was still closeted with Burnamy, and pretend that she had not known they were there. But a soberer second thought than this prevailed, and she told the girl who it was that was within and explained the accident of his presence. "I think," she said nobly, "that you ought to have the chance of going away if you don't wish to meet him."

The girl, with that heroic precipitation which Mrs. March had noted in her from the first with regard to what she wanted to do, when Burnamy was in question, answered, "But I do wish to meet him, Mrs. March."

While they stood looking at each other, March came out to ask his wife if she would see Burnamy, and she permitted herself so much stratagem as to substitute Agatha, after catching her husband aside and subduing his proposed greeting of the girl to a hasty handshake.

Half an hour later she thought it time to join the young people, urged largely by the frantic interest of her daughter. But she returned from the half-open door without entering. "I couldn't bring myself to break in on the poor things. They are standing at the window together looking over at St. George's."

Bella silently clasped her hands. March gave cynical laugh, and said, "Well we are in for it, my dear." Then he added, "I hope they'll take us with them on their Silver Wedding Journey."

———————————

Booksophile

Your Local Online Bookstore

Buy Books Online from

www.Booksophile.com

Explore our collection of books written in various languages and uncommon topics from different parts of the world, including history, art and culture, poems, autobiography and bibliographies, cooking, action & adventure, world war, fiction, science, and law.

Add to your bookshelf or gift to another lover of books - first editions of some of the most celebrated books ever published. From classic literature to bestsellers, you will find many first editions that were presumed to be out-of-print.

Free shipping globally for orders worth US$ 100.00.

Use code "Shop_10" to avail additional 10% on first order.

Visit today
www.booksophile.com

www.ingramcontent.com/pod-product-compliance
Lightning Source LLC
Chambersburg PA
CBHW032229080426
42735CB00008B/778